MIDNIGHT MURDER

The murder of Madame Bourchaud was puzzling. She was found dead in her bedroom, despite the police cordon around her hotel and private detective Lionel Crane being stationed outside her room during the previous night. A fabulous pearl had been stolen, ripped free from the silver chain around her neck, which also showed bruises, suggesting strangulation. But then it was discovered that she had died from arsenic poisoning . . .

DONALD STUART

MIDNIGHT
MURDER

Complete and Unabridged

LINFORD
Leicester

First published in Great Britain

First Linford Edition
published 2012

Copyright © 1935 by Gerald Verner
Copyright © 2011 by Chris Verner

British Library CIP Data

Stuart, Donald.
  Midnight murder. - -
  (Linford mystery library)
  1. Detective and mystery stories.
  2. Large type books.
  I. Title II. Series
  823.9'12–dc23

  ISBN 978–1–4448–0970–1

Published by
F. A. Thorpe (Publishing)
Anstey, Leicestershire

Set by Words & Graphics Ltd.
Anstey, Leicestershire
Printed and bound in Great Britain by
T. J. International Ltd., Padstow, Cornwall

This book is printed on acid-free paper

1

In the night

'Hello, Herrick, what's up?'

Lionel Crane stopped his car alongside the figure in the bowler hat, and smiled at his old friend. Detective-Inspector Herrick walked over to the side of the pavement. It was a bitterly cold night, and the Scotland Yard man was wrapped to the chin in an immense overcoat, out of which his stolid face jutted bleakly.

'Burglary,' he snorted. 'May even be murder!'

Crane's face lighted up with interest, and Harry Pollard, Crane's young partner, who was beside his friend, leant forward excitedly.

'When did it happen?' Crane asked.

'It hasn't happened,' was the morose reply; 'but it is going to, unless I can put a stop to it somehow.'

Detective-Inspector Herrick scratched

his head as he spoke, and gazed thoughtfully into his hat. His saturnine face was more morose than usual, and, in the strong light from a nearby streetlamp, Crane could see the very real worry in his eyes.

'I wondered what you were doing outside a private hotel at this time of night,' put in Pollard, indicating the pillars with their emblazoned notices: 'The Devon Private Hotel'. 'I thought that Mrs. Herrick must have locked you out, and that you were looking for a bed,'

Young Pollard chuckled, and Herrick grimaced at him.

'What's the trouble, Herrick?' Crane asked.

'Our friend the Phantom Stealer again,' was the grim reply.

'The 'Phantom Stealer'? That's a new name to me. Who is he?'

'Don't ask me. He's a new thorn in our sides. He cropped up soon after you went abroad, and he's been leading us a fine dance ever since. He's cleverer than a bagful of monkeys, and has us guessing far more often than we care to confess.'

2

'What's his speciality?'

'Pearls. He never goes after anything else. Information came through this evening that he was after a pearl in this hotel.'

Herrick gazed doubtfully at the shabby building. 'It seems a queer place to find a pearl worthy of a master-crook's attention,' he added.

'Someone's pulling your leg,' suggested Pollard.

'Maybe. But I've had warnings about the Phantom Stealer before, and they've never proved wrong. I believe the fellow likes us to know of his intentions beforehand, and then to pull off his show under our very noses.'

'Have you made inquiries about a pearl in there?' questioned Crane.

'I have, and the only pearl that I can find is the kitchen maid. Her name is Pearl.'

He accepted a cigarette from Crane, and lit it thoughtfully. 'I've a cordon around the place,' he continued, 'and I've interviewed everybody in the building. They're just the usual bunch of old maids, retired army officers, and clergy-men's widows.'

'You are sure that you saw them all?' insisted Crane.

'Yes; if the manager can be believed.'

'What time did you get here?'

'An hour ago.'

Crane stared at the pillars thoughtfully.

'Everyone was in bed, I suppose?' he hazarded.

'Yes; some trouble I had getting them up, what's more.'

'Perhaps you did not get them all up. Hotel managers are considerate beings where good residents are concerned. May I butt in, Herrick, and interview the manager?'

Herrick grinned, his morose unhappiness leaving him miraculously.

'I was hoping you'd do something like that, Crane,' he confessed, 'but I didn't like to suggest it. This Phantom Stealer has been getting on my nerves, and this case is worrying me. I've got a hunch — I can't explain it — that he is going to pull this thing off tonight. I'm not given to fancies, you know that, Crane, but

4

— well, I've got a presentiment of trouble.'

Pollard chuckled, but Crane took the detective-inspector seriously.

'I'll come right on in at once,' he said, as he climbed out of the car and followed Herrick up the steps.

Herrick and he had been friends for many years, and he knew the Scotland Yard man's sterling qualities. He knew that, once Herrick was on a trail, he was more tenacious than a bull-dog, and there were occasions in the past when he had risked his life unhesitatingly for Crane. He, however, laid no claim to extensive reasoning power. He required a keener brain to show him a line of action, then nothing short of death could keep him from following it to its end. Crane had a very real affection for Herrick, that was returned in full by the Scotland Yard man.

Herrick led the way into the hall, and a sleepy porter was dispatched for the manager, who proved to be a small, fat German, who came down in a very bad temper at being disturbed for a second time.

'He haf seen everypoddy,' he declared, pointing angrily at Herrick.

'Are you sure?' said Crane.

'Do I not tell you? You haf wokened me, and now you haf called me a liar.'

Crane smiled, and the man was somewhat mollified by the frank good humour of it.

'Vat do you vant?' he asked grumpily.

'I was wondering,' confessed Crane smoothly, 'whether in the carrying out of your duties, and in the interests of certain of your visitors, who were perhaps very tired, you had refrained from fetching one or two favoured ones from their beds.'

'I haf told him — '

'I know, but may I see the visitors' book?'

With an angry grunt the small man fetched the book and pushed it into Crane's hands. It was a much-thumbed book, scrawled all through with many signatures, an excellent textbook for a student of handwriting. In a quiet voice, Crane read over the names, asking Herrick at each name whether the owner had been present.

His eyes, however, covertly studied the manager.

'Madame Marie Bourchaud,' he repeated, noting again the nervous look that crossed the manager's face. 'I think,' he went on, 'that we might see her again.'

The manager swore, and hammered angrily on the desk,

'I tell you he haf seen everypoddy,' he shouted. 'Madame Bourchaud is sleeping! If she come from bed again, she vill leave. You vill haf make all my peoples leaf me!'

'Before you call her,' the private detective went on in an even voice, 'you will tell us something about her. Her signature is interesting. It is a well-trained hand, and denotes breeding and power. I should be inclined to think that it is slightly disguised. If you look, Herrick, you will see that it is rather forced. There is not the easy, accustomed flow that denotes a signature that has become second nature to its writer. One sees this hesitancy in the signature of a newly-married woman.'

He smiled at the manager.

'Perhaps,' he suggested, 'madame is newly married?'

'She iss not,' was the reply. 'She iss widow, perhaps. She haf no husband here.'

'Ah!' said Crane. 'Tell me, who is she? Where did she come from?'

The steely grey eyes hypnotised the angry manager into replying. An angry retort trembled on his lips, but he realized that here was a man that one dare not trifle with. There was no kindlier man living than Crane, but on occasion he could be implacable.

'I know noddings,' pleaded the German. 'She come to this hotel mit luggage, She vant room. There iss room. She take room. She stay vun, two, tree veek. She pay in advance. Vat more vant you?'

Pollard hurriedly turned a laugh into a cough, and avoided Herrick's eye. The manager was inexpressibly comic as he waved his hands before Crane and danced with rage in front of the quiet figure of the detective.

'But where did she come from?' Crane asked.

'Of dat I know noddings.'

'How did she come? In a taxi?'

'No; mit her feet.'

'And her luggage?'

'Mit an outside porter.'

Crane drummed thoughtfully on the reception desk before him, and considered the angry face.

'Do any of the people here know her?' he asked at last.

'No; all know noddings,'

'I see.'

Crane turned away and paced the hall, while Herrick questioned the manager and drove him to the point of distraction.

'But she iss poor lady!' he wailed at last. 'She haf been ill today. She vant go bed early. Am I dog that I vake her!'

'Dog or no dog,' decided Herrick, 'you'll send right up and wake her now.'

The manager made to refuse, but he caught Crane's eye, and with a surly nod sent the sleepy porter up to the lady's room, informing the world in general at the same time that he was ruined.

Crane continued walking up and down while they waited, leaving Pollard and

Herrick to soothe the manager's ruffled feelings. Pollard mentally considered what sort of woman this was going to be who could so thoroughly cower the irascible little manager. He decided that she would be elderly, proud and overbearing. When she eventually appeared, he stepped back in amazement. She was tall and dark, and she swept down the stairs like a queen. Even Crane found himself staring rudely, for she was one of the most beautiful women that he had seen in the course of his career.

'Messieurs want me?'

She surveyed them haughtily, and there was no snobbishness about it. It was the natural hauteur of a woman used to subservience from all around her. Herrick backed hurriedly away and snatched off his bowler hat. Crane stepped quietly forward.

'But, yes, madame,' he replied in French, deciding that he would have to work on a bluff. 'We have received warning that an attempt is to be made tonight on the jewel that madame carries. This gentleman is from Scotland Yard; I am a private detective. We are here to protect madame and her jewel.'

'But what jewel?' protested the French woman. 'I am but a poor woman. I have no jewel.'

Nevertheless, Lionel Crane's keen glance had not missed the cloud of apprehension that came to her eyes, nor the instinctive manner in which her hand went to her heart.

'Madame,' he asked, 'may I have a word with you in private? Believe me, it is only your interests that I am considering. I will keep you from your sleep but one moment longer.'

'No!' She stared at him proudly and coldly. 'I know not what you want. I have no jewel.' She turned to the manager, who was nervously rubbing his hands together in the background. 'Who are these persons?' she demanded. 'Is my rest of so little importance that I am to be disturbed in this manner? Did I not tell monsieur that I have a headache?'

'Madame!' he began to bleat, but she silenced him with a wave of the hand.

'Messieurs have either mistaken me for

11

someone else, or they are impertinent.' A sudden, brilliant smile softened the words.

'I will return to my room. Goodnight.'

Without looking back, she sailed up the stairs. Herrick wiped his perspiring forehead with a large handkerchief.

'We've done it this time,' he groaned. 'Got a poor woman out of bed for nothing.'

Crane shook his head, and led the way outside.

'Herrick,' he said impressively, 'you've got to guard that woman with every facility under your control. She has a jewel that is more valuable to her than her life, but, for some reason, she dare not confess its existence. The Phantom Stealer has got wind of her treasure, which must be a pearl, as you say that he never goes after anything else. I am afraid that your hunch is going to prove correct tonight. Madame is hindering us on every side, but guard her we must, despite her assertion that she does not possess a jewel.'

'She deserves to lose it,' decided

Pollard, who objected to the lady's haughty treatment of his chief.

Crane shrugged his shoulders.

'She would probably be happier without it,' he said, 'for, by the look of her, she gets very little sleep through worrying over it. It is our job, however, to protect it, and it's up to us, eh, Herrick?'

'You can count on me,' replied Herrick. 'I've already got a cordon around the place, but there are so many snags, especially when the person to be protected treats one like something that the cat has found,'

'Put men on the landing by her door,' said Crane. 'Under her window; in the next rooms on either aide, if possible. No one must get near to her.'

Herrick grunted again, and after a few words with the manager, went off to carry out Crane's suggestions; then he joined Pollard and Crane outside Madame Bourchaud's door and they settled down to pass what little remained of the night in waiting.

The hours dragged slowly past. The hotel was soon silent as it retired once more to its rest. Pollard could hear a tap dripping somewhere, and a sound of heavy snoring from one of the rooms. He amused himself by guessing when the clock in the hall was going to strike. A recreation that culminated in his betting himself a hundred to one that six o'clock must strike, as it seemed eternity since he had heard five, He checked the time by the luminous dial of his wristwatch, and discovered that five had struck only eighteen minutes before.

The morning light found the detectives still in their places, and shone greyly on their unshaven faces.

'We've wasted our time,' began Herrick, but Crane's hand closed on his arm and silenced him. The door of madame's room opened, then closed sharply again.

'It was a woman,' declared Herrick, in a hoarse whisper. 'Her ladyship herself.'

Ten minutes later it opened again, and she swept out, dressed for travelling in a fur coat and a dark hat and veil. In her hand was a small dressing case.

She passed the detectives with her face

haughtily averted, and sailed on down-stairs.

'One of my men will keep her in sight,' whispered Herrick, in reply to Crane's mute query. 'We'd better hang on here, eh?'

'Yes; once she's well away, we'll have a look at her room. The chances are that she has hidden the pearl there. After all, she must realize that she stands more chance of having it stolen when she carries it about with her.'

A few moments later they were joined by a diminutive man in blue serge, whom Herrick addressed as Harris. He had been stationed outside the window on a small balcony.

'Couldn't see in,' he told them, as Herrick pushed open the door and they entered the room. 'She kept the heavy blinds pulled, but I kept my ear glued to the window, and she slept hard all night. Snored something awful!'

Crane's eyes narrowed. Madame Bourchaud had not been the type of woman to be given to heavy snoring. He was so thor-oughly keyed up and on the alert that he

15

was ready to seize on anything that was at all suspicious. He was on the point of questioning Harris, when Herrick gripped his arm. The big detective's eyes were bulging, and his face had paled strangely.

Crane followed the direction of his horrified stare.

The counterpane on the bed hung down to the floor, but it did not quite conceal all that lay beneath.

'A hand!' whispered Pollard in horror.

In one stride Crane crossed the room and drew up the coverings.

'It's her!' cried Herrick. 'He's got her — '

Crane bent over the woman and studied the vivid bruises on her neck. When he turned back to the others his face was set grimly, and his voice, when he spoke, was harsh with feeling.

'Your hunch was right, Herrick,' he muttered. 'It is — murder!'

2

The pearl of Andapore

'She got away!'

The hoarse voice rang out sharply in the hush that had fallen on the small room after the discovery of the body. The detectives swung round as one man, and stared at the dishevelled figure in the doorway.

'Greene!' exclaimed Herrick. 'What on earth — ?'

Detective-Sergeant Greene fingered a bruise on his cheek. His lips were swollen, one eye was closing, and he had an ugly cut on his head; also his clothes were dusty and torn, while his hard felt hat was merely a battered wreck.

'She got away,' he repeated dully. 'I followed her out to the Harrow Road by Notting Hill and Ladbrook Grove, she walked all the way. Then she turned into Kensal Green Cemetery. As I went after her round one of the big tombstones, she came for me. Like a fury, she was; and she knew how to use her fists. I'm a bit, of a boxer myself, sir,' — he studied his battered fists — 'but she had me beat. Could hit like a male, and was a light on her feet as a fairy.

'I tried to reason with her, and dodge, but she just came after me. Then she beat me to it, and got in two stunners, which had me out. By the time that I was up again she had gone.'

'Ah!' snorted Herrick. 'And I suppose you came straight back then to tell us how ill-treated you were?'

'Not I, sir. I didn't have a chance. People had seen the fight, and a woman cried out that I had tried to rob the lady. A big crowd gathered — goodness knows where they all came from. She set 'em on me, and I got mobbed. By the time I got clear there was no hope of finding the woman in black. She had vamoosed with plenty of time to spare. I made inquiries, but no one had seen her, or so they said.'

'What time was this?' Crane asked.

'It was twenty to seven as I turned into

the cemetery,' replied the disgruntled plainclothes man. 'And just five to when I started my inquiries.'

Crane nodded and smiled encouragingly at Greene, for it was obvious that the man was feeling his position keenly. He stared shamefacedly at the floor while he was speaking, and tried not to see the amused grins on the faces of his colleagues.

'Don't take your defeat too much to heart,' advised Crane.

'It's being knocked out by a woman that riles, sir,' confessed Greene. 'It ain't never 'appened before.'

Crane shook his head,

'That was no woman. That was our friend the Phantom Stealer,' he declared.

'You think so?' said Herrick. 'I was wondering myself.'

'I am pretty certain of it,' continued Crane. 'He must have hidden himself in here while Madame Bourchaud was downstairs; then robbed and killed her, counting on making his escape disguised in her clothes.'

'I suppose he got in while we were

talking to her in the hall?' suggested Herrick.

'He may have,' agreed Crane. 'Although it is quite likely that he had been there for some time. A man like that must have infinite patience.'

'He's certainly got nerve,' broke in one of the detectives. 'It took more than ordinary courage to dress himself in his victim's clothes, and walk calmly out past the police, and then to waylay and knock out a police officer.'

'He's a cool customer, right enough.'

The police surgeon was another old friend of Crane's, and they examined the body together. Death had apparently been caused by strangulation. The unfortunate woman's neck was bruised and cut by sharp fingernails. She had put up a frenzied struggle for life, and her face was set in a frozen stare of horror acid despair. One of her hands still gripped the remains of a silver chain that passed round her neck.

'She must have had a bag suspended around her neck with the pearl in,' decided Crane. 'A simple way of carrying valuables, to which women are much given. She clutched it, and her assailant broke the chain to get her treasure from her. See how it has marked her neck.'

Along the back of the slim neck was a vivid weal to show where the chain had bitten in owing to the force with which it was being pulled.

'An odd little chain,' remarked the doctor. 'A series of three links and a cube of solid silver. Not much intrinsic value, of course, but slightly out of the ordinary.'

Crane nodded,

'You can trace the pattern on her neck. May I take a paring of a fingernail from the other hand, Herrick?' he asked. 'She scratched her adversary pretty thoroughly, and there is both hair and flesh imbedded in these long nails. I am always interested in hair, as you know. One can work up a description of a man from a sample of his hair.'

While Crane and the doctor were examining the body, Herrick arranged for thorough inquiries to be made around Kensal Green Cemetery for any information concerning a woman in black.

'He will have to go somewhere to change back into his ordinary kit,' he pointed out. 'The only thing is to trace him to some lair. It is more than likely that he has one in that vicinity.'

Police photographers set to work and made pictorial records of every aspect of the room in which the tragedy had taken place, and detectives searched it from end to end for any chance clue that the Phantom Stealer might have left behind. Crane left the doctor after a while, and, assisted by Pollard and Herrick, made a preliminary inspection of the dead woman's effects. Each drawer was carefully emptied and searched. A quantity of rich clothes was disclosed, and a few pieces of fine jewellery.

'All these clothes are old,' decided Crane, 'and have been altered from time to time. At one time Madame Bourchaud must have been a rich woman, and able to gratify her every whim, but recently she has come down somewhat in the world. The majority of the things that have not yet been altered were the latest fashion about six years ago. All, you will observe, have had the dressmaker's name removed. She undoubtedly had something to hide, and she feared that she might be traced by her clothes.'

A heavy leather writing case, that had cost much money at some distant date, proved to contain a few receipted bills from the hotel, and a quantity of pawn tickets. Nothing else.

'She was getting broke all right, Li,' exclaimed Pollard. 'By these tickets she must have been getting rid of her stuff at a furious rate, and living on what she raised.'

Herrick took the tickets and handed them to his men.

'Inquire into these,' he ordered. 'I'll let you know what the pawnbroker has to say,' he added to Crane.

Crane thanked him, and took a final look round.

'I'll get off home to Welbeck Street,' he decided, 'and have some breakfast. You might keep me informed of any developments, if you will, Herrick.'

'You're very quiet, Li,' said Pollard, as the two speeded home in the car.

'I am trying to place a face, Harry,' was the reply. 'I have seen Madame Bourchaud before somewhere, or a photograph of her, but I can't quite place where.'

'She made one think of a queen,' suggested Pollard. 'Is that suggestion any good to you?'

'I had thought of that, and when we get back I want you to go through my albums and study all the Royal personages of all countries with extreme care. She certainly had the appearance, accent, and air of a Frenchwoman, but most Continental Courts are run on the same lines, and French is pretty generally spoken. Pay particular attention to all pictures of the old Russian nobility.'

'Right you are, Li.'

Crane retired to his room with a pipe on their return to Welbeck Street, where Pollard settled down with the albums of photographs. The time passed slowly, and it seemed as though his toil was going to be in vain. Crane came in after a while, and settled himself in an armchair, from which comfortable position he proceeded to fill the room with smoke. To the casual eye he was asleep, for his eyes were closed and his whole body relaxed, but the tireless brain was going over every point in the dramatic crime that was under consideration.

'Nothing doing here, Li,' declared Pollard at last. 'I've been through the lot.'

'Try the actresses,' suggested Crane, without opening his eyes.

'Nix again,' reported Pollard some time later. Crane did not reply for a short while. He knew that Pollard could be trusted on the work in hand, for the young man had an excellently trained memory for faces, and, had there been a picture bearing any resemblance to Madame Bourchaud in the collections that he had been through, he would have noted it at once.

'The Rogues' Gallery,' ordered Crane at last.

Linker, his manservant, put his head round the door at the moment.

'I 'ave rung the gong for breakfast,' he said, 'but you'll be lettin' it grow cold, as you always does, I suppose. It ain't a cook you want, sir, it's a tin opener! Hot, cooked meals is wasted on you.'

He sniffed disdainfully at his master, but brightened as Crane's austere face softened in a smile.

'I'll put it back in the hoven if you're busy,' he added, somewhat mollified.

'If you will, Linker. We will just finish what we are doing.'

But Linker was to waste many vain regrets on that breakfast, for it was not destined to find its way into Crane and Pollard. Much was to happen before they ate another meal in their Welbeck Street dining room.

As the door closed on Linker, Crane leant forward with a gleam in his eye and pointed to a portrait in the book on Pollard's lap.

'There she is!'

'In the Rogues' Gallery,' exclaimed Pollard excitedly, 'on the very first page that I opened at. That's what you call Fate, Li.'

'Read it out, Harry.'

While Crane made notes, Pollard obeyed.

'Name: Madeleine Gaudriol. Wife of Paul Gaudriol.

'Nationality: French.

'Age: Born January 23rd, 1899. Height: 5ft. 8ins.

'Build: Slender. Hair: Dark brown.

'Complexion: Fair. Eyes: Dark grey. Nose: Long, straight. Lips: Medium. Mouth: Medium, finely formed. Ears: Small. Scars, etc.: Thin white scar from base of left ear to base of neck. Prominent vaccination marks on left arm. Small finger on left hand bent towards next finger owing to previous fracture. Gait: Smooth, with longish strides.

'Habits, peculiarities, etc.: Her every action denotes excellent breeding, etc. Impersonates Royal personages, Russian refugees, etc. Very heavy tea-drinker, and addicted to 'Monovitch' Russian ciga-rettes. Has an instinctive impulse to wave away unwelcome conversation, etc., with a peculiar sweep of the hand. Mixes very little with fellow crooks, and has participated but little in her husband's crimes.

'Places frequented: The opera, horse

shows. She is an excellent horsewoman. Auction rooms, where she occasionally buys pearls, the only jewels in which she takes any real interest.

'Record: The wife of Paul Gaudriol. Before her marriage to him in 1919 nothing is known of her. He appeared with her in London at the close of that year, and brought off eight sensational burglaries in the next eighteen months. Has very little to do with actual operations, beyond posing as a foreign noblewoman to gain the confidence of intended victims. Lived richly with her husband, for whom she entertains very real love. Disappeared after Paul Gaudriol's capture and sentence to seven years in 1922. No sign of her has been seen since.

'It fits her all right, Li,' cried Pollard, when he had finished reading. 'You remember the airy gesture with which she silenced the manager, and I noticed the scar, too.'

'Yes; it fits her all right, and it fits in to everything else. I don't know if you remember, Harry, but Paul Gaudriol was 'put away' for the theft of the Andapore Pearl.'

Pollard nodded in great excitement.

'Yes; I remember. There was great excitement over it because Gaudriol stole it from the Maharajah of Andapore, and the maharajah fairly raised London. They caught Gaudriol, but I don't remember what happened to the pearl.'

'It was never found.' Crane puffed quietly at his pipe. 'Gaudriol must have had an opportunity to pass it to his wife, and she contrived to disappear. I can understand her agitation and fear to disclose the existence of the pearl. Not only were the police and the maharajah's agents after it, but Gaudriol's companions swore that he had double-crossed them, and vowed that they would find the pearl. So the poor woman had the whole underworld after her, besides the law.'

Crane studied the description again, his brow creasing with deep thought.

'It is a pity that this is such an inconclusive description, Harry,' he said. 'It must be the worst in our collection.'

'I know, Li, but I remember now, it was

29

an awful job trying to collect information about the woman. Gaudriol had kept her away from all his pals, and she appeared so seldom, and had had her tracks so well hidden, that it is a wonder that we managed to collect as much information about her as we did.'

'I must have another look at the body,' decided Crane, 'Just to make sure of the identification, and must have a word with Herrick to see what he has on the police records concerning Madeleine Gaudriol. Something tells me that we are up against a stiff proposition in this case, Harry, and that there is more in it than the Phantom Stealer with his hankering for pearls.'

'Had I better read up about the Pearl of Andapore?' began Pollard, but Crane held up his hand for silence.

From the hall came the sound of Linker's voice raised in expostulation.

'I tell you 'e's 'avin' 'is breakfast, or 'e ought to be if 'e wasn't too busy.'

The words ended with a startled exclamation and the sound of the manservant sitting down rather hurriedly.

Running footsteps sounded on the stairs and a voice called:

'Mr. Crane — Mr. Crane!'

The private detective reached the door and flung it open just as the intruder reached the landing. The man bounded past him into the room, where he paused doubtfully. He was a tall, thin individual in the dishevelled remains of a smart grey suit. He had an ugly cut on his head that was bleeding profusely, and in one hand he still clutched a neat, plated revolver.

'He's after me!' he cried. 'He's after my pearl!'

'Mix a stiff whisky-and-soda,' said Crane to Pollard, 'while I go and see who is after him.'

By the time that Crane had returned, Pollard had got their visitor somewhat calmed. He was sitting in a chair with his drink in his hand, and so great was his agitation that the liquid was in danger of slopping out of the glass.

'There is no one outside,' said Crane quietly. 'Whoever was after you must have decided not to follow you in here. Do you mind telling me who you are, and what the trouble is?'

The other made a desperate effort to pull himself together.

'I am afraid that I made a very melodramatic entry, Mr. Crane,' he confessed; 'but I am not accustomed to alarms and excursions. To be set upon in one's own study and nearly brained, and then to have a revolver held at one's head is disturbing to the steadiest of nerves, and I work too hard with my brains to have steady nerves.'

'I see,' said Crane quietly. 'But may I ask you who you are? That will be the easiest point from which to start your story.'

The other managed to smile.

'Of course, that is simple; my name is Malcolm Page. You may have heard of me?'

'I've read your books,' said Pollard, looking with interest at the writer of the most realistic detective stories that he had ever read.

Crane also nodded.

'I also admire your crime stories, Mr.

Page,' he said politely.

Malcolm Page swelled visibly with pride.

'That's splendid praise from an expert,' he said. 'As for my adventure this morning, I am almost inclined to think that my imagination has been playing tricks with me. I have written of such a happening often myself. I shall have to begin at the beginning, though, and to do that I must explain that I am a collector. I don't specialise in any line, but just pick up whatever takes my fancy. I was in India last year and secured a truly beautiful pearl. It was my companion all the way home on the ship, and, besides its intrinsic value, I became very attached to it. I am like that. I can become great friends with inanimate objects. They become almost human to me.

'Sometime back I received an anonymous letter threatening the theft of my pearl. I tossed it into my wastepaper basket.

'This morning I was finishing the correcting of some proofs in my study, when I was struck a violent blow on the head. I happened to reach sideways at the moment, so the blow missed the mark that it was aimed at, and, in place of rendering me unconscious, gave me this scalp wound.

'I sprang to my feet, and found standing over me a tall figure in black, with a mask over the face, and wearing a cap — well, it was shaped like a motorist's helmet, only made of black silk.

'The moment that I turned round my assailant leapt backwards and dashed out of the door. I reached for my revolver and followed him. Out in the corridor I regretted my precipitate action, for he came for me again. I will confess that I turned and fled. I ran downstairs and, the front door being open, out into the street. I live only a few doors away, so I came straight here.'

'What was your assailant like?' asked Crane.

The man wrinkled his forehead.

'It is really impossible to say, for he was so completely masked, and everything happened so quickly. I got the impression of a very tall man with a rather small head and long, slim feet in smart black shoes with crepe-rubber soles.'

'It is unusual to have black shoes with crepe soles,' muttered Crane. 'Possibly he had blackened a pair of brown. He was unfortunate in coming up against you, Mr. Page, for your work would naturally make you observant of small details like that. Is there anything else that you can tell us?'

'I am afraid not.'

'About your pearl? Is it still safe?'

For answer Malcolm Page reached into his pocket and drew out a small chamois-leather pouch, which he emptied into his hand.

'What a beauty!' exclaimed Pollard, gazing with great interest at the white miracle in the author's palm.

Crane took it between finger and thumb and examined it critically.

'You certainly have a wonderful pearl here,' he told Page. 'It must be one of the most perfect pearls in the world. I expect that there is a story behind it. Pearls always have their stories.'

Page laughed.

'I expect that there has been a great deal of blood besides mine split over that one,' he agreed. 'But, as far as I am concerned, there is very little to it. I bought that pearl in Medows Street, Bombay. I had to pay for it, of course.'

Crane was about to ask a further question, when a knock at the door materialised into Linker.

'A note,' he snorted. 'Stuck under the door. Nobody would think as this was a civilised country, they wouldn't. What is letterboxes for, I should like to know?'

Crane split the envelope open, while the others watched him. The note was short and to the point.

★ ★ ★

'I have won once, Crane. The second round, you win. But I will get Page's pearl yet. I'll race you to it.
'THE PHANTOM STEALER'.

36

3

At Malcolm Page's House

'I should like to have a look at your study,' Crane said suddenly, as Page was preparing to go. The author turned back at once.

'Look here,' he said, 'my breakfast will be ready. I am late for it already, but my housekeeper is used to my erratic meal hours. Why don't you and your partner come and eat with me? Then you can take your time to look over the scene of the crime. Or, perhaps I should say, the scene of the attempted crime.'

'I should like to,' said Crane; and Pollard chuckled.

'Linker will be wild,' he told his master. 'He'll buy a tin-opener and never give us another hot meal.'

'Ho!' said Linker, as they passed him in the hall. 'Goin' hout, are you, sir. Ho! An' me with breakfast in the hoven! This

'ouse will be called the Tramps' Eatin'
'ouse it will. Makin' 'ot meals for tramps.
I gives it all to tramps,' he added as a
Parthian shaft. 'They enjoys it! Appreci-
ates good cookin', they does, which is
more than some people do.'

Page wanted his guests to have their
food straight away, but Crane asked to see
the study first. It proved to be a big, airy
room at the top of the house, lighted by a
large skylight.

'That must be how he got in,' said
Page, pointing to the open skylight. 'I
have often thought how easy it would be.
In fact, I have used the idea once or twice
in a story.'

Crane inspected the polished floor with
care. Plainly to be seen were the imprints
of the toes of a pair of shoes with rubber
soles, denoting the skill with which the
Stealer had dropped lightly to the
ground.

'Are there any steps?' the detective
asked. 'I should like a look up there.'

'The library steps will do the job nicely,
I think,' replied Page. 'The library is just
through here.'

While Pollard was aiding the author to wheel in the steps, Crane once again studied the floor. With his magnifying glass in his hand he went over it carefully, starting in the middle of the room and working in all directions, ending at last by the entrance to the library.

'These things are hard to push into here,' declared Page. 'Their accustomed place is the library, and they never leave there.'

The cumbersome ladder was arranged under the skylight, and Crane mounted. He paused on the top step, and examined the glass and the sides of the glass trapdoor. In the dust were the plain imprints of a man's fingers.

'Careless!' muttered Crane. 'Rather surprising for a man as sharp as the Phantom Stealer. Ah! And here are his footprints. Quite clear again. One set coming to the trap — that is all. He did not go this way. He must have followed you out by the front door, Page.'

The author and Pollard had followed the famous detective up the steps, and they stood beside him as he surveyed the view from the roof.

'There is only one window that overlooks this,' Crane pointed out. 'Do you know whose house that is?'

Page shook his head.

'I know none of my neighbours,' he confessed. 'I work rather hard, and at odd hours, so I have not much time for making friends. We can soon inquire, though. Would you like to go round now? There is a chance that someone might have seen a man on the roof.'

'Yes, we must do that, but first I want to discover how he got up on the roof.'

Crane followed the tracks to the edge, where the question was soon answered. A rainwater pipe led down into a small yard. The veriest tyro could have climbed it.

'Builders ought to be made to cover rain-pipes with barbed-wire or something!' snorted Page. 'That's a positive invitation to a crook.'

'We must find our way down to that yard,' decided Crane. 'We should find some trace of our man down there.'

At the entrance to the courtyard, when at last they found their way to it, was an old man with a red face, who stood placidly puffing at his pipe. He shook his head at each of Crane's questions.

'I ain't seen no one,' he declared. ' 'Arry, did you see a bloke climbin' the rain-pipe?' he shouted.

Another ancient workman came from a doorway, and also shook his head.

'We bin 'ere most of the mornin', sir,' to mumbled, 'and there ain't bin no acrobatics on rain-pipes 'ere.'

'When were you away?' asked Crane.

'We was away for abaht ten minutes at nine o'clock.' The workman hit his thigh a resounding smack. 'Bill, that was it! The cove wot gave us the price of a pint. 'E must 'ave gone up the pipe while we was away.'

Crane's eyes narrowed at the clue that had at last come to their hand.

'What was the man who gave you the price of a drink like?' he demanded.

'Tall gent with a beard.'

'An' dark glasses,' supplemented his companion.

'What was he dressed in?' questioned Crane.

'Lemme see. Ah, a mackintosh! One of them long rubber ones.'

'What sort of hat?' prompted Pollard.

'Grey felt. Yes, that was it — grey felt, like you 'ave on yourself, with the bound edge.'

'Did you see the colour of his hair?' went on Pollard.

Both workmen scratched their heads. Bill at last decided that it had been black hair, while Harry plumped for grey. Crane mentally allowed for the lack of observation of the average man. The chances were ten to one that the hair had been neither black nor grey. He nodded to Pollard, who went on with his questions.

'Anything peculiar about his nose?' he asked.

'It must 'ave cost 'im a mint of money,' decided Bill. 'It were a whackin' big beak, an' as red as a fire-engine.'

'Hands?'

''E wore grey gloves,' declared Bill.

'Yes,' echoed Harry. ''E wore gloves.'

'Was he a fat chap?' asked Pollard.

'No; thin, but 'e 'ad plenty of go about

'im. Not skinny, you know.'

'What was he wearing on his feet?'

'Boots!' said Bill, with a pitying glance at Pollard, as much as to say: 'What do you expect him to wear on his feet — a hat?' More than this they could not tell Crane took over the questioning, and cross-examined them skilfully, but a more conducive description of the Phantom Stealer he could not get.

Thanking the workmen for their information, and rewarding them, he returned with Page and Pollard to the author's house. On the way they looked at the house with the window that looked over the skylight through which the Stealer had made his entry, but found that it was empty.

'We seem to bang our heads against a brick wall every way we turn,' grumbled Page. 'As fast as we stumble on to a clue, it leads to nothing. What's the next move?'

'Breakfast,' replied Crane simply. 'I for one am decidedly hungry, and it is after ten o'clock. If you are sure that we won't be putting you out, Page?'

'My dear chap, you are welcome!' replied the writer. 'This morning has been a pleasure to me. I have written about imaginary detectives so often, that it has been a great thrill to work with a real one.'

As they sat at the excellent meal, which Page provided, Pollard could not help but notice Crane's preoccupied air. The young man knew his partner well enough to be able to read him. He realized that something about the events of the morning was troubling Crane. He questioned Page about his books and his collection, striving assiduously to give Crane a chance to think without too many interruptions.

'I was thinking of this pearl of mine,' Page said suddenly, turning to Crane; 'also one or two other prize bits in my collection. This morning's attack has rather unnerved me, and I don't feel safe about them. I shudder, as it is, to think of the risks that I have been running.'

'Why not put them in the bank?' suggested Pollard.

'No; I am so used to having them by

me that I should be acutely unhappy without them. I am like a miser. I like to get all my treasures out in the evening and gloat over them. What I was wondering was if it would be possible to get special police protection?'

Crane considered the matter.

'You could arrange for the constable on duty outside to pay particular attention to your house,' he suggested. 'Or, as Pollard suggests, you could put them in a bank or safe-deposit somewhere. After all,' he added, with a smile, 'it would be possible to take them out once a day, and — as you say — gloat over them.'

Page laughed.

'I am not really as bad as that,' he said defensively. 'Perhaps I am superstitious, but I feel somehow that all my luck would desert me if I sent my collection out of the house. Couldn't I arrange for a Scotland Yard man to stay in the house with me, or something like that?'

Crane shook his head.

'That would be a bit beyond the scope of Scotland Yard, I am afraid,' he replied, with a smile. 'They provide detectives for weddings and functions like that, but it would be asking too much to expect them to keep a man here with you on the off chance that an attempt might be made on your collection in the future.'

'But what about that note that you got? The Phantom Stealer definitely threatens to steal my pearl.'

Crane studied the author thoughtfully for a while.

'I'll tell you what I'll do,' he said, at last. 'I'll be seeing Detective-Inspector Herrick shortly about a case that I have in hand. I'll mention your request to him, and see what can be done. I am afraid that that is all I can promise.'

Crane was very silent as he and Pollard drove down to Scotland Yard to discover what fresh news Herrick might have. They found the inspector behind his desk, staring thoughtfully at the wall, and at his favourite recreation of sharpening pencils. When Herrick wanted to think out some knotty problem he was never happier than with a bundle of pencils and an old razorblade. He would sit by the hour pointing his pencils with extreme care, and when his supply ran out he would break those that he had done so as to have a fresh lot to attend to.

He waved Crane to a chair, and carefully finished the point that he was working on. As he cut he talked.

'No news of the woman in black,' he reported. 'She was seen by no one after leaving the cemetery. If it was the Stealer, he must have faded into thin air. I have had the most exhaustive inquiries made.'

Crane picked up one of the finished pencils and drew circles on a sheet of blotting paper.

'Has it struck you, Herrick,' he asked, 'that in a cemetery there are vaults? Few things could be easier than to slip into the entrance to one of those family mausoleums, slip off a fur coat, a lady's skirt and hat and emerge as a totally different being?'

Herrick finished his point with more care than usual.

'I'm a fool!' he said simply, reaching for the phone. 'I'll send a man down to comb out the cemetery. He might find the discarded clothes.'

After speaking to a subordinate, he drew a list towards him, and addressed Crane.

'I have had a report on those pawn-tickets. The things were pawned in the name of Bourchaud. They comprise — ' He hurried through a list of jewellery and other valuables. 'Madame Bourchaud must have been a rich woman once upon a time.'

'She was until her husband went to gaol,' said Crane.

'What!'

'I said until her husband went to gaol,' repeated Crane, and proceeded to enlighten Herrick with regard to their discoveries of the morning.

'Madeleine Gaudriol!' exclaimed the inspector. 'By Jove! He comes out of Parkmoor shortly, you know. Someone will suffer for last night's work. They were, by all reports, the most devoted couple imaginable. It is funny, but you often find that with a man like Gaudriol — a thorough-paced crook, but devoted to his wife, and a most exemplary family man. I never saw Madeleine Gaudriol, but I have heard late companions of his speak of the pair of them.'

'Gaudriol must be shadowed from the moment that he leaves the prison,' decided Crane. 'He might lead us to our quarry. The Phantom Stealer is a daring foe, Herrick. Not content with his haul last night, he made another attempt this morning.'

'Rather!' cut in Pollard. 'He nearly killed Malcolm Page, the author, and attempted to steal his pearl!'

Herrick broke a pencil point, and had to reach for his safety-razorblade.

'Tell me about it, Crane,' he begged.

Briefly Crane gave him a resumé of the attack on the writer, omitting nothing, but Pollard could see that something about the whole story was troubling him.

'I promised Page that I would speak to you about police protection,' he concluded. 'I thought that perhaps you might like to see him as you are so keen on laying the Stealer by his heels. Page might be able to help us. He is a clever chap, and his writing has fitted him to lend a really useful hand in an affair like this.'

Herrick was about to reply, when the phone-bell rang shrilly. The inspector's face as he answered it expressed first interest, then surprise, then a comical sort of horror. It became mottled, and the eyebrows almost disappeared in the thick hair.

'Crane!' he almost whispered, as he laid the receiver down, 'that was the doctor speaking. He has just examined the body of Madame Bourchaud — Madeleine Gaudriol.'

'Well?' asked Crane. 'What has he found?'

'She did not die of strangulation! Those marks on the neck show that great violence was used, but she was dying before her throat was seized.'

'Dying!' Crane was on his feet now. 'Herrick, what do you mean?'

'Dying, Crane. The doctor has found distinct traces of poison! There is no doubt but that poison was administered to her at some time yesterday. It was working when she was attacked, and she died in the robber's hands, but she died from the effects of the poison!'

For a moment the detectives stared at one another.

'Poison?' gasped Pollard. 'But why should he try to strangle her if he had already poisoned her?'

Crane shook his head.

'Something tells me, Harry, that the Phantom Stealer received as great a shock as anyone when the woman died. He meant to throttle her into unconsciousness, but he did not kill her.'

'Then,' muttered Herrick, 'who did?'

'That,' declared Crane, 'adds one more mystery to this case. The Phantom Stealer tore the pearl away from her — he has confessed to that in his note to me — but the question remains — who poisoned Madeleine Gaudriol?'

4

A race against time

For quite an appreciable time there was silence in Herrick's office. The Scotland Yard man sharpened his pencils moodily, while Lionel Crane drummed on the desk with the tips of his fingers, and stared out of the window with unseeing eyes.

'We have one line to work on,' Crane muttered at last, 'and that is Gaudriol. When he hears that his wife is dead, nothing will keep him from those responsible, and he may lead us to the murderer. When is Gaudriol to be released, Herrick?'

Without replying, the inspector reached for the phone again, and was soon in communication with another department.

'Thanks!' he said at last. 'No, that's all I want for the moment.'

He turned to Crane.

52

'Gaudriol will be released this afternoon at two,' he said quietly. 'Queer, isn't it, the way things fit in? It's getting on for one now.'

Crane made a rapid mental calculation before he replied.

'An hour in which to do fifty-eight miles. That means that we must break all law of speed. The road is good once we get clear of London. It can be done, I think. How are we off for petrol, Harry?'

'Tank almost empty, Li. Shall I nip down and fill up?'

'Yes, and make any necessary adjustments as quick as you can, Harry. We daren't have a breakdown on the road. If we lose sight of Gaudriol, we will lose our only hope.'

While Pollard sprinted out to the car, Detective-Inspector Herrick reached for his bowler-hat.

'Wait for me, Crane!' he shouted after the detective's hurrying figure. 'I'm in on this!'

Crane ran an expert eye over the engine of the car, while Pollard attended to the replenishing of the petrol-tank and

Herrick fussed in the offing. The few adjustments necessary were soon made, and with Crane at the wheel the big car slipped silently through the traffic. The private detective knew his London, and, what was more important, his car. With the practised skill of a born driver, he took inspired chances, and kept Herrick's heart in his mouth.

'Gosh!' gasped the latter, gripping his hat, as they slid miraculously between two buses, cut across the front of a line of traffic, and nipped down a quiet side-road. 'If Mrs. Herrick could see me she'd be writing out her claim for the insurance money on my life.'

Once clear of the traffic, Crane let the huge machine out and roared along the Great West Road. An A.A. scout signalled a frantic warning of a police-trap, and a 'bus driver almost fell out of his seat in an attempt to pass on the same advice, but Crane kept his foot down, and the speedometer needle mounted steadily. Beside his friend, Pollard stared ahead, his whole mind centred on the car, which he knew so well. His accustomed ears were listening to the roar of the great engine, and seeking for any unfamiliar note.

The big machine was running at its best, so that even Pollard, who was hypercritical where cars were concerned, smiled a grim smile of satisfaction. Assisted by a mechanic, he had taken the mighty engine down a few days before, and he felt that his labour was being well repaid.

Clutching feverishly to the side of the tonneau and his hat, Detective-Inspector Herrick marvelled at Crane's driving, and revelled in the exhilarating speed. Cars appeared in the distance ahead of them, only to disappear again, leaving a blurred impression of scared-faced people craning out and shouting. A policeman yelled and held out a hand, but Crane never slackened his speed, and the man in blue made a wild dive into the ditch.

'I'll square things!' screamed Herrick. 'Keep going!'

At the next crossroads tragedy seemed imminent, but the machine's brakes shrieked, and she rocked madly towards the hedge. With fine judgment, Crane skidded her round and whipped between two lumbering steam engines with trailers.

Herrick let out a yell, then turned and howled his opinion of them at the engine drivers. On tore the car. Villages cropped up, to drop behind. Startled folks dashed to the doors and windows; police wrote furiously in their notebooks and burnt the telegraph wires with messages concerning the speeding car.

At last Crane swung into the long, straggling main street of Parkmoor, and drew up in the shade of some trees not far from the walls of the prison. The clock on the dashboard made it four minutes to two.

Crane was the first to get out, and, as he did so; he made a rapid change in his appearance. A few expert twists to his not too smart clothes, and a touch or two from the make-up box that was an essential part of the car's equipment, and no one could have recognized the detective. In his place was a cadaverous individual in a dusty check cap and an oily raincoat with a tear across one pocket.

'You must take over the car, Harry,' he decided. 'Get back to London and wait for a message from me.'

He looked questioningly at Herrick who scratched his head and studied first the make-up box and then his bowler-hat.

'I'm not a quick-change artist,' the Scotland Yard man decided eventually, 'and I'm known personally to Gaudriol. Still, I'd like to be in on this show. He's a dangerous customer, and I'm not going to leave you to tackle him alone. What am I to do, Crane?'

Crane shrugged his shoulders.

'You can keep attention from me,' he declared, 'by openly getting on to the train after Gaudriol and travelling to wherever he gets out. Then leave him to me. I shall want you waiting at the Yard in case I require help. Gaudriol is cunning. It won't do for both of us to fall into a trap.'

The clock on the prison gate struck two very shortly after Crane had settled himself into a convenient vantage place.

57

Almost at once the gates opened and a warder came out with a tall, lean man in a blue suit, which hung loosely on what had once been a gigantic frame. The prisoner, a dark, foreign-looking individual, looked eagerly around. Crane could see his face clearly, and he noted the surprise turn to dismay and then resentment. With a muttered curse, the man nodded to the warder and slouched off down the hill to the town.

'He was looking for his wife,' Crane muttered to himself. 'What he'll do when he discovers the truth is beyond reckoning, but there's going to be trouble!'

Gaudriol made his way straight to the railway station and boarded the London train, his release having been so timed that there was one waiting at the platform. Crane entered a compartment somewhat further down the train, and he noticed Herrick shaking hands with a puzzled stranger. The stranger's face was turned away from Gaudriol, so that the cheerful farewell appeared quite natural to him. He only heard Herrick's booming:

'Thanks for a grand time, old chap!'

The train was moving, and Herrick had flung himself into a compartment before the stranger had collected his wits enough to make any reply.

At Waterloo, Gaudriol took the Tube, with Crane close behind him. A perky little man in pince-nez took the seat next to Crane in the tube, and a note changed hands:

Browne was at Waterloo. Have put him on to aid you.
HERRICK.

Gaudriol left the Tube at Lancaster Gate and hurried to the Devon Hotel. Crane and Browne waited in the street at a discreet distance from the door of the hotel and one another. In the interval each made changes in his appearance, so that it was two very different men who were ready to take up the trail of Gaudriol again.

The wait was a long one. When at last Gaudriol came down the steps, he staggered like a drunken man, and his face was as white as chalk. He paused for a moment on the pavement, rubbing his head in a bemused way. Then the sign over a public house caught his eye, and he hurried across and in through the swing door.

Browne passed close to Crane, and, as he did so, muttered:

'There is another man behind with a car sir. If he takes a taxi, hop into a black Vauxhall that will draw up beside you, I'll get on the luggage-rack and under the rug.'

Gaudriol was not long having a drink to aid him to pull himself together. In a very short space of time he walked steadily out and hailed a passing taxi. Lionel Crane attempted to get close enough to hear the address that he gave to the driver, but it was impossible without arousing suspicion. As the taxi started off again, a dark car passed slowly in front of Crane, and, sheltered from the occupant of the taxi, the detective swung himself aboard and settled down to watch the car ahead.

The chase that followed was a stern

one for the quarry chose the roads with the most traffic in them, and kept issuing instructions to the driver to swing down side streets The man at the wheel of the Scotland Yard car was an expert at his job, and drove like an inspired being, but it was all that he could do to keep the other in sight without disclosing his purpose.

The car was very ordinary in appearance, and he generally contrived to keep two other vehicles between him and his quarry, but still Crane decided that Gaudriol was too sharp not to have realized that he was being followed.

'Keep straight on,' he ordered his own driver, 'and about fifty yards ahead draw to the side of the road. Then get out and fiddle with your engine. I shan't want you any more. I'm going to transfer into a taxi. Tell Inspector Herrick that I will 'phone him as soon as possible.'

At a moment when the traffic was thickest, and when his movements were well cloaked with many vehicles, Crane slipped from the Vauxhall and into an empty taxi, which was held up in the same block.

'Keep that taxi, Number XL2774, in sight,' he commanded. 'There will be a good reward for you if we don't lose sight of it.'

In the shelter of his cab, Crane once again made changes in his appearance, never taking his eyes off Gaudriol's car as he did so. They turned at last into Oxford Circus, and the first cab stopped by the Underground station.

'Straight on!' ordered Crane, slipping a note on to the seat beside his man. 'Don't stop until you are a good two corners away. Thank you for the way in which you have helped me.'

Once again he left his car while on the move, and lost himself in the traffic. When he at last reached the pavement, Gaudriol had collected some change from his driver and was turning into the station. Crane waited until the Frenchman had booked to Shepherd's Bush, and then took a ticket himself at one of the automatic machines.

At Shepherd's Bush, Gaudriol walked rapidly down to Goldhawk Road Station and took a ticket to Regent's Park. Once again Crane was behind him, and both changed at Hammersmith. Outside Hammersmith Station Gaudriol threw away his Regent's Park ticket. After standing by the roadside in deep thought, Gaudriol sprang forward and hurled himself on to a 'bus. Crane was too experienced a tracker to dash after the same 'bus. Instead, he stepped on to the running board of a tradesman's van and gave the driver an unexpected present to keep behind the 'bus.

'Wot's 'e been doin'?' asked the van driver.

'He's a convict from Parkmoor,' explained Crane. 'I want to keep him in view, that's all. We'll grab him later on. He may lead us to his pals.'

'Ah!'

Crane made a wild leap from his perch almost opposite the Underground station in Kensington High Street, and narrowly missed annihilation by a car behind, but he was just in time to follow his quarry to the ticket office. Once again they both entered the same train, Crane with a ticket the whole way, as he had been unable to discover where the Frenchman had booked to.

At each station Crane watched the passengers disembark, but there was no sign of Gaudriol until Praed Street, when he caught a fleeting glimpse of him in the crowd. The detective hurried from the train and added himself to the throng, but when he reached the lift it was shut in his face.

'Next lift!' barked the attendant. 'No more in 'ere!'

Without pausing, Crane dashed wildly up the stairs, but when he reached the top, even as he had feared, there was no sign of his quarry. In vain he described his man to all the loungers around. None had seen him. One or two told the detective bluntly that they had more to do than watch the people come out of the station. All Crane's afternoon and evening work had been for nothing. Owing to a simple matter like the capacity of a lift he had lost his man.

'I'll ring Herrick,' he decided, and he gave the inspector a brief account of his chase around London. 'Lost him in the end!' he snapped. 'But there is no sense crying over spilt milk. You might warn all your men to keep an eye out for Gaudriol. Broadcast his description, and send men who know him to all his old haunts. 'Phone me if anything comes in. I'm going home.'

When at last Crane made his weary way into his own house, Pollard met him in the hall.

'There's been a chap waiting for you for fifteen minutes, Li,' exclaimed Pollard. 'I gave him a whisky as he seemed all broken up.'

'What name?' asked Crane wearily. 'I don't feel like interviewing anyone at the moment. I am tired out.'

'He wouldn't give his name, Li.'

The door of the consulting room opened and a man hurried eagerly out.

'Mr. Crane!' he called eagerly. 'Is that Mr. Lionel Crane?'

Standing with his hand on the door handle was Paul Gaudriol.

★ ★ ★

Detective-Sergeant Greene searched Kensal Green Cemetery in his slow, methodical manner, but it seemed that his efforts were to be in vain.

'He must've taken the togs along in that handbag,' he decided. 'Still, I had better go through every one of these places. Ah!'

The detective concealed his portly form behind a gravestone as quick as a flash. Greene had a trained mind, and his powers of observation had been brought to the highest pitch of efficiency. While trailing the Phantom Stealer in his disguise as the woman in black, the Scotland Yard man had noted a slight peculiarity in the gait of his quarry. An almost unnoticeable twist of the left foot while walking and a slight jerk in setting the foot down. It was the type of idiosyncrasy that would have passed unobserved to the average passer-by, perhaps even to the trained man, but Greene, as he put it, specialised in feet.

Walking rapidly down the path was a tall, slim man in a dark suit. Most of his face was concealed by a gigantic, bushy beard, and despite the unsavoury weather, he wore sunglasses.

Greene noted all this in one comprehensive glance, but his attention concentrated on the man's left foot. The twist was identical, also the odd jerk at the end of each stride.

While Greene watched, the bearded man stooped down by a most elaborate edifice and remained hidden for a brief moment. When he appeared again he was stuffing something into one of the capacious pockets of his coat. After cautiously looking to left and right, but missing the concealed detective, he turned once more down the path. Greene hesitated. In his pocket was a revolver. It would be the work of a moment to transfer it to his quarry. Then he could arrest his man for illegally carrying arms, and remove him at once to the police station. Once there, he could depend on Herrick to see that he did not get away again, provided that he was indeed the Stealer.

Before Greene had a chance to make up his mind, his quarry hailed a passing taxi and set off down Harrow Road. Greene flung himself into another. The chase was not a long one, for the first taxi drew up before a house in a narrow street only three turnings from where it was originally engaged. The man with the beard paid off his driver and admitted himself with a latchkey. Greene noted the address and hunted vainly for any sign of a telephone. Being of a cautious disposition, his intention was to ring Scotland Yard and inform Herrick of the enemy's latest move before taking any step on his own. His search for a 'phone failed to disclose one, so he cautiously approached the house into which the man with a beard had entered.

It was an old-fashioned place with an area, so after a brief hesitation Greene crept down the area steps. The kitchen into which he looked was empty. The door gave no trouble to his experienced fingers, and he soon slipped the lock. The room itself proved to be unfurnished, and by the dirt and cobwebs had not been used for a very long time. The back stairs proved to be equally uncared for.

With extreme caution the Scotland Yard man made his way up them and gently opened the door at the top.

With a cry he attempted to shut it again, but a long knife, gripped in a black-gloved hand, flashed downwards.

Greene had a fleeting glimpse of a black-masked face; heard a snarl:

'You'd spy on me, would you!' and then he crashed backwards down the stairs.

With a hysterical laugh the figure in black flung the knife after the body of the detective and turned on his heel.

* * *

Crane was still closeted in his study with Paul Gaudriol from Parkmoor when the telephone-bell rang.

'Inspector Herrick wants you, Li,' called Pollard. 'He's in an awful stew about something.'

Crane hurried to the 'phone, and Herrick's voice, shrill with excitement and concern, came to him.

'Crane? That you? The Phantom

69

Stealer has got Greene! He was found in the cemetery — I had sent him there to hunt for any clues among the vaults. Poor old Greene — one of my best men. Stabbed through the heart!'

5

Gaudriol's story

Crane turned to the ex-convict who was watching him curiously.

'You were just saying that you do not suspect the Stealer of the murder of your wife — that killing is not in his line,' he said. 'Well, he has killed this time. A Scotland Yard detective has been murdered in Kensal Green Cemetery.'

Gaudriol leapt from his chair.

'Murdered! How, sir? Shot?'

'No; stabbed through the heart.'

Gaudriol shook his head in a worried way.

'That doesn't sound like the Stealer, sir. Of course, I never came up against him. He only began operating after my time, but I heard a great deal about him from men in there with me.' The Frenchman's eyes met Crane's squarely, and he betrayed no emotion as he discussed his profession. 'I took an interest in him, sir, for after all, we were what you call birds of a feather. I also specialised in jewels, and had a weakness for pearls. Curse all pearls — you have a saying in your language that pearls mean tears. It was a pearl that caused the death of my Madeleine — '

He stopped speaking and turned his head quickly away. Crook though the man undoubtedly was, Crane admired him for his feeling, and there was something very likeable in Paul Gaudriol.

'What have you heard about the Phantom Stealer?' Crane asked.

Gaudriol hesitated.

'I am a sportsman, Mr. Crane,' he said at last, 'and I have never betrayed a man yet, but I will tell you what I know of the Stealer because I must find who killed my wife, and to do that I must be frank with you. You, I know, will not betray anything that I tell you in confidence, and will not press me to tell you anything that I deem it better that you should not know. Is that so?'

Crane nodded.

'We can help one another, Gaudriol. For that reason I am glad that you decided to come to me. I shall respect your confidences, but for your part, I want you to leave out nothing that might help me in the handling of this case.

'I shall have to get along to Scotland Yard and inquire into the death of this detective,' the famous detective added, 'but before I go I should like to know all that you can tell me about the Phantom Stealer.'

There was only the merest suspicion of an accent in Gaudriol's voice, it being obvious that he had been to great pains to suppress it. He spoke slowly and carefully, and his alert eyes studied the listener keenly, backed by a clear brain.

'No one knows much about the Phantom Stealer,' he began. 'As far as I could gather, he commenced by stealing the Rosenbaum Pearl — a treasure that I had had my eye on for a long while — in broad daylight. He was scarcely known to members of the profession. No one has seen him without his peculiar hat, shaped like a racing-helmet, and his black mask.

On the few occasions that he has had to enlist recruits for a job that was too big for one man, he has picked his assistants with care. Two men I met who had worked with him, but neither could give a clearer description than that he was tall and thin, and wore silk clothes of black, and a mask. He is as strong as two men, and has an extraordinary knowledge of pearls. He is a cultured man, and can mix with any society.

'The general impression in the underworld is that he is a swell gone wrong — a man with the entrée to the best houses. The man who was with him when he took the Dalrymple Pearl declared to me that the Stealer knew the house intimately, and referred in a sneering voice to Lord Dalrymple as 'Old Freddie',

'I questioned him carefully about peculiarities, but beyond the mask and his clothes generally no one had noticed anything.'

'What about his voice?'

'Rather high-pitched.'

'His walk?'

'A free, swinging stride. He is as light

74

on his feet as a cat, and as silent.'

'Has anyone noticed his hands?' Crane asked.

'No; he always wears black gloves.'

Crane was silent for a moment, while Gaudriol racked his brains for any further details about the Stealer.

'Has he got any recognised headquarters?' the detective asked.

'No.'

'Where does he pick up his men, then, at any time that he needs them?'

Gaudriol hesitated, then he smiled rather grimly.

'I suppose I had better tell you, Mr. Crane, but I want you to play square by me. At the back of the Canton Chop-suey in Water Causeway, just off the East India Dock Road, is a large room filled with junk. In reality, all these old casks and oddments form walls, and within the big room is a smaller one. Li Chang — or, rather, the men behind him — makes a tidy income out of that room. I used to meet my assistants there.' Gaudriol smiled again. 'I am going to tip off all my pals that you know of its existence, Mr.

Crane,' he concluded. 'But I can promise you that not one of them will put the Stealer wise, or any men who have worked for him at any time.'

'What men have worked for the Stealer?' Crane asked next. 'Could you give me the names of some of them?'

'You will use this information only to catch the Stealer?' warned Gaudriol. 'You won't pull in any of his men? We are after the Phantom Stealer, not his tools. Some of them are pretty good sticks, men that I can't understand working for such a rogue.'

'To the best of my power, I will not take unfair advantage of what you tell me,' promised Crane. 'I cannot say more than that.'

Gaudriol hesitated, but Crane possessed the knack of inspiring confidence, and the ex-convict took a pencil and paper and wrote down the names of all those that he had heard were given to working with the Phantom Stealer.

'I must be going along to Scotland Yard now about this fresh murder,' said the detective. 'I want to keep in touch with you, Gaudriol. Where will I be able to find you?'

Gaudriol gave the address of a lodging-house.

'Be careful how you communicate with me,' he warned. 'I took a very big risk in coming to see you, but I was told at the Devon Hotel that you were on the case, and I wanted first-hand information. Also, I made up my mind that if any man could help me to get justice, you could. It is unlikely that I was followed, although I was suspicious once or twice, notably of a Vauxhall car that seemed to be following my taxi; but I twisted and turned around London, and I am sure shook them off. If any of my people knew that I had come to you, my life would not be worth that!' He snapped his fingers. 'Their consciences are overburdened, and they would suspect me of selling them.'

Crane saw the ex-convict to the back door.

'What can I do to help?' Gaudriol asked. 'I can't hang around idle.'

'Mix with your old pals,' advised the detective. 'As I told you, I myself suspect that the Stealer did not kill your wife. Someone else had administered poison to her. You are certain that under no circumstances would she commit suicide. I want you to look up every man who knew that you had the pearl; all those who threatened to avenge themselves on you at your trial.'

Gaudriol nodded, his long jaw setting.

'I'll look into that, Mr. Crane,' he promised. 'I'm going to think over what you said tonight. I may have something to tell you the next time we meet. Goodbye, and thank you! You — you are being very good to me. It means something in this world to know that one will be given a square deal.'

Crane found a message from Herrick awaiting him at Scotland Yard to say that the inspector had gone on to Kensal Green, and asking Crane to follow.

The famous detective was admitted by the police who were guarding the entrance, and hurried over to a group by one of the tombs.

'I'm glad you've come,' cried Herrick. 'This gets more and more puzzling every minute. I want you to have a look at the body and the signs on the ground, and tell me what you think.'

Crane bent over the still form of Greene. The detective-sergeant was lying on his back, with one arm bent under him, and his legs stretched out. On his right temple was a vivid bruise.

Crane laid a tentative hand on the left arm, which had been bent peculiarly across the chest.

'Arm broken,' he said simply.

Cautiously Crane moved the stained and cut jacket and peered at the ugly wound above the left breast. He studied it in silence for a few minutes, then, with the police-surgeon's assistance and per-mission, probed it.

'A sweeping, downward blow did this,' he decided. 'You can see where the edge of the knife has cut the flesh above. There is not as much blood around here as I should have expected.'

The detective rose to his feet and began to study the ground by the body. After a few moments he turned to Herrick, who was watching him curiously.

'You asked for my opinion,' he said. 'Well, it is that this man was not killed here. My reasons for are: first, that a man struck a downward blow with great force — a blow that pierced the heart — would be liable to fall on to his face; secondly, the arm under the body is not broken, though, if he had fallen on it, it must surely have been. On the other hand, his left arm is broken. Wherever he was killed, he fell on to his left arm and fractured it. Then, again, he is lying on his back and yet he has a bruise on his temple; a bruise, what is more, that was made against some dusty object. You will see the dust and a fragment of cobweb on the skin.'

Crane turned again to the body and examined the clothes.

'The dead man has been in some disused shed or room, you can mark the thick dust on his boots and the cobwebs that have clung to his clothing,' he said.

'I had decided that he was not killed here,' replied Herrick, 'but simply because there are no signs of a struggle.'

Crane nodded.

'You can see a line of footprints here,' he said, leading the way to the nearest side path, 'which are deeply impressed and close together — a man walking heavily and carrying a burden. If you were to make inquiries, I have no doubt but that you would discover that a man walked through here with a sack, and stopped for a brief moment by this grave.'

'It would take some nerve in broad daylight,' exclaimed the doctor.

'What makes you say a sack, Crane?' asked Herrick.

Crane shrugged his shoulders.

'It would be a convenient article for the job, and, besides, I noticed a quantity of brown fibres on the victim's clothes.'

Herrick and Crane went together to each of the entrances and carefully cross-examined the occupiers of the nearby shops and houses and any loafers that were around.

'I saw a big man with a sack,' declared the owner of a greengrocer's. 'A gent 'e were, with a beard an' black glasses. 'E passed along 'ere about 'alf an hour ago, an' I saw 'im cross the road.'

'From which way did he come?' asked Crane.

The man pointed up the road.

'You're sure?'

'Yes, sir, 'e came down the road that way; I saw 'im plain.'

The two detectives walked slowly in the direction indicated, and many of the shopkeepers attested to having seen the bearded man with the sack. After they had gone a couple of hundred yards, they could find no one who had noticed their quarry.

'He must have come from a side street further back,' declared Crane. 'We'll retrace our steps to the point of our last successful inquiry, and try the side streets from there.'

At the first two corners on each side they were unsuccessful, then an old woman with a jug vowed that she had seen the man exactly as they had described, come around the corner by which she was standing and gossiping.

'Baht 'alf-hour past, sir,' she declared. 'Saw 'im plain, I did. Funny lookin' cove wi' an 'airy face.'

They took the turning indicated and found themselves in a residential street of somewhat decayed houses.

'We'll work our way along, inquiring from the servants and any people that we meet,' decided Crane. 'Servants see most of what goes on from kitchen windows.'

His plan proved successful, for at the first kitchen at which they inquired, a fat cook, with a pleasant, red face, recognised their man at once.

'I've seen 'im often, sir. We calls 'im Old Beaver. 'E lives at number fourteen, but 'e ain't got no servants there, and I ain't never seen no smoke comin' from the chimneys.'

She insisted on climbing her area steps to point out Number Fourteen, and stood to watch the detectives approach it. Herrick went down to the kitchen entrance, while Crane tried the front door. The famous detective was just about to use an instrument on the lock, when Herrick called him.

'The kitchen door is unlocked,' Herrick called softly. 'We can get in this way.'

Just inside the door both stood still,

with the knowledge that their search was ended. They were on the scene of the murder of Detective-Sergeant Greene.

At the bottom of the backstairs was a large pool of blood, while in the middle of the floor lay a revolver which Herrick recognised as belonging to the unfortunate sergeant.

'They killed him here,' said Herrick quietly.

Crane studied the stairs, going over them with his powerful lens.

'Greene entered the same way as we did,' he explained, 'and made his way up the stairs.' Herrick walked softly after Crane as the detective ascended step by step. At the door both hesitated. Very cautiously Crane opened it. The hall beyond was empty. Crane bent down and examined the floor.

'This is where Greene was killed,' he decided. 'The Stealer was waiting for him, and stabbed him as he opened the door. That accounts for the wound. Greene was standing on the second step, so the Stealer struck from above. Greene fell forward, hit his temple against the doorjamb, and pitched down the stairs. You can see where the cobwebs have been disturbed here, and the distinct traces of a heavy body rolling from step to step.'

'What about the Stealer?' asked Herrick.

'He went down to the kitchen, either immediately after striking the blow, or some little time later; here are his tracks. We know what he did then.'

Herrick nodded.

'Put the body in a sack, and took it down to the cemetery. He's a cool customer all right.'

'We had better search the whole house,' said Crane. 'There is just a chance that our man may have left something of interest behind. It is unlikely, but one never knows. He must have made up his mind to abandon this den, or I feel sure that he would have been more careful about clearing up traces down in the kitchen. He must have left in a hurry, and only a short time ago, so he may have overlooked something.'

'It is extraordinary how careless a crook can be,' said Herrick hopefully. 'Shall we begin upstairs and work downwards?'

Crane agreed to this, so the two made their way to the top of the house. The whole of the top floor was deep in dust. It was evident that the Phantom Stealer had never even been up there. Still, the two detectives examined each of the empty rooms.

'Second floor,' said Herrick.

Here they were more successful, for in the third room that they examined, they found traces of occupation.

Along one wall was a camp bed of a cheap make, by which stood a card table and a deckchair.

'Does anything strike you about his furniture?' asked Crane.

'Cheap,' replied Herrick. 'You could buy the lot, including the Primus stove, for just over a pound note.'

'It can tell us more than that,' said Crane. 'It proves that this house was a close secret of the Stealer's, which he'd disclosed to no one. Every one of those bits of furniture is folding and could be brought here in a light car and carried in and upstairs by one man. This was the

Stealer's secret lair, which he disclosed to no one.'

Herrick nodded his head sagely.

'That's it,' he declared. 'Pretty Spartan, wasn't he? A bed, a table and a chair — finish!'

'I should say that this was only a temporary hiding place,' replied Crane. 'A sort of half-way house, where he could change from one disguise to another, or get a few hours' sleep. We will find, unless I am mistaken, that he has a real home elsewhere, a place where he is a pillar of respectability.'

While they talked the two detectives went through the few effects that the Stealer had left. There were two grey blankets on the bed, and two sheets.

'Excellent linen,' remarked Crane feeling the texture of one of the latter. 'Our man does not believe in the coarse touch of blankets. There is no common touch about him. He is a man who is accustomed to the good things of life. These sheets prove that. The old type of crook, sprung from a lowly origin, never mind how rich his crimes made him, would not have dreamt of providing himself with sheets in a temporary camp. He would have had blankets to keep him warm, and that would be all.

'You will notice that there is no pillow,' continued Crane. 'Perhaps I am wrong, but I reason from that that the Stealer has a car, and formed the habit of bringing a car-cushion up to form a pillow.'

Crane turned to the table.

'Not much there,' remarked Herrick, 'an old newspaper — eight days old, and nothing else.'

Crane laughed and took out his lens.

'One never knows what there is not quite visible to the naked eye,' he pointed out. 'Here we are, right away, this circular stain on the green baize was made by a bottle. A simple test or two, and we would know what our man was in the habit of drinking. Then the burns around the edges, where he has carelessly left his smokes, from time to time, they are broader than would be made by cigarettes. I would say that he smoked cigars. Also, you can smell the cloth. He smokes strong cheroots — Burmahs, I should say.

'These stains on the cloth are not ordinary paint, and here is a slight powdering of rouge. He has placed his make-up box here.

'Now, look at the deckchair, there is a greasy patch on the canvas. Sit there for a moment Herrick — ah! Your head is a good three inches below the mark. Now we'll use our sense of smell again.'

Crane sniffed at the canvas, and nodded his head thoughtfully. He turned to Herrick who was watching him with amused interest.

'I can tell you something about our man now,' he declared. 'I will describe him to you: He is tall, above the average — you are five-eleven, I believe, Herrick, so we can take it that he is at least six-foot one. We have been told that he is thin by more than one witness. He has large feet, and is addicted to pointed shoes.

'The beard that has been mentioned we can dispense with, as we have discovered that he possesses a make-up box which has been used frequently. He is a well-educated man with an inbred taste for good things; smokes Burmah cheroots; and possesses a car with a loose cushion, which is soft enough to use as a pillow. As for his drink, if you smell very carefully at that stain on the cloth, you will be able to pick out the scent of brandy, so we can take it that he is given to brandy, and not the more common man's drink — whisky. Then — my nose again! — he has the bad habit, in my opinion, of making lavish use of brilliantine. A very good brand, by the delicacy of the aroma scented with violets.

'You can sort those facts out as you like, and take them in conjunction with what we have already been able to discover concerning him, and I think that we can say that we are getting nearer to our man.'

'I'll keep those points concerning him in mind,' agreed Herrick; 'and we'll try to add to them from time to time.'

Crane picked up the newspaper, and studied it curiously.

'It is strange that a man should have a newspaper eight days old,' he remarked, 'when we know that he has been here since then. This paper has also been folded rather strangely, and has been well thumbed. I should be inclined to think that this paragraph has been read frequently. Listen to this, Herrick.'

In an even voice he read from the paper, but his eyes glinted with excitement.

*   *   *

' "Sale of famous pearl. Actor's purchase. Mr. Walle Frayne, the well-known Shakespearean actor, has added to his priceless collection of jewels the famous Rose Pearl. This beautiful treasure, valued at an incredible figure, was formerly the property of the Countess of Wigmouth, but it is rumoured that it has now passed into the hands of Mr. Frayne, and there is little reason to doubt Dame Rumour on this occasion, although both the countess and Mr. Frayne refuse to discuss the matter",'

Herrick whistled.

'He'll be after that!' he exclaimed.

'I think he will,' Crane assented. 'And

91

there lies our next move. It is only a quarter to eight now. I will hurry round to Mr. Frayne's flat and have a talk with him. By a fortunate chance I have met Frayne on one or two occasions, so it will be simple for me to convey a warning to him, and to ask him to cooperate with us.'

'I'll get on back to Scotland Yard,' said Herrick. 'I suppose that there is nothing else that I can do?'

Crane hesitated, and stared thoughtfully at the camp bed.

'A man of the Stealer's class and type has a single-track mind in some respects,' he muttered. 'When it comes to buying things, habit makes them go to one of the big stores — the place where they always deal. I would suggest that you take this stuff round to Harridges, the Naval and Military — places like that — and see if you can trace the purchaser.'

Herrick admitted the possible clue, and promised to see what could be done; and the two detectives parted at the door of Number Fourteen.

6

The Rose Pearl

Walle Frayne had a spacious flat in a large detached house in Chiswick. A pompous manservant in clothes that appeared too large for him on account of his angular figure, admitted Lionel Crane.

'There is a gentleman with Mr. Frayne, sir,' he said. 'If you would not mind waiting in this room for a few moments I will take your card to him.'

Crane had a long memory, and could safely boast that he never forgot a face. It was impossible for him to fit a name immediately to every face on his seeing it after a long interval, but he would know at once if he had met the owner before. In the case of Frayne's manservant, Crane could remember no name, nor the occasion on which he had run against the man, but the long, very lined face, and thin, nervous hands had attracted his attention on some other occasion. He also did not fail to note the start with which the man read the name on his card.

'I'll have to ask Frayne a few questions about you, my friend,' he decided. 'I don't remember you on my previous visit to this flat.'

'That you, Crane?' boomed the actor's rich voice. 'Come right on in here. I've only old Malcolm here. We're discussing pearls.'

'We seem doomed to meet,' prattled Malcolm Page, the author, as he and Frayne came forward to welcome the famous detective. 'You know, Mr. Crane, I was telling Frayne of my adventure, and the way I dashed into you — I was warning him to be careful of the Rose Pearl — '

The author stopped suddenly and turned to Frayne with a comical look of dismay.

'My tongue has run away with me again, I am afraid,' he apologised.

The actor, a giant of a man, with very dark hair and a strong mobile face, laughed with real enjoyment.

'Don't worry about Crane, Mal, old son. He won't pinch the Rose Pearl. Besides, half London knows by now that I have it; so I'm going to make it a secret no longer. I doubt if anyone would have the nerve to steal it. This house is well strung with burglar-alarms, and the pearl never leaves my person; also I carry a gun, which I know how to use.'

He laughed again.

'You know,' he confessed, 'that the pearl is giving me great pleasure — besides the joy of possessing one of the treasures of the world. It is adding the spice of adventure to my life. I eye everyone with suspicion, and spend spare moments devising the most amazing schemes. For one thing, I have just told you that the Rose Pearl is on my person, but I defy anyone to find it. They can strip me and go over my clothing with a knife — cut it all to shreds, if they like, including my boots.' He grinned at Crane. 'I believe that the heel of a boot is a favourite hiding place for such things, isn't it, Crane? Well, my boots would disclose nothing.'

'You've been taking a leaf out of the Kaffirs' books on the Rand goldmines,' suggested Page, 'and cutting your skin to make a pocket for it.'

'Too uncomfortable for me,' chuckled Frayne. 'I'd rather lose my pearl than go to those lengths.'

'I shall have to do something like that,' decided Page. 'I am really worried about mine, because I am very fond of it. I had thought of having a slot made in my shoes, but, after what you have just said, Frayne — '

The actor's mighty laugh echoed through the room once more, and Crane laughed with him. While Page stared at them both in worried perplexity.

'It is all very well for you to laugh,' he told them, 'but you have not been attacked by this Phantom Stealer. I have.'

'I wish I had,' declared Frayne. 'I'll guarantee that there'd not be much Phantom Stealer left. Why, the very name is childish!'

'I thought it rather good,' replied Page. 'In fact, I wish that I had thought of it for a book. He is a stealer, and he's certainly pretty phantom-like. Nobody knows him. He just takes his booty from the fat necks of plump women and vanishes.'

'If you call yourself a plump woman,' chuckled Frayne.

'It is about the Stealer that I came to see you, Frayne,' cut in Crane, seeing that Page was in danger of losing his temper under the other's raillery. 'I have reason more than to suspect that you are to be his next victim.'

In a few words he told of the newspaper that he and Herrick had discovered; refraining, however, from any mention of the place where it was discovered, or the events leading up to the discovery.

'I knew it!' cried Page. 'I knew that he would come after you! Crane, what are we to do? There are two of us now.'

'Do?' boomed the actor; 'why, teach the bounder a lesson. I'm glad that he's after me. He will find that he has struck a stiff proposition.'

He stopped suddenly, and turned to the manservant, who had appeared in the doorway.

'Well, Pearson, what is it?'

'Mr. Wilson and Mr. Harley, sir.'

'Come in, you chaps!' shouted the actor. 'Come and hear the latest. You are just about in time to witness the signing of my will.'

'Why, what's up, Walle?' asked the first of the newcomers, a tall, elderly man in a velvet coat, baggy grey trousers, and immense black bow-tie, whose hair seemed rather at variance with his youthful-looking face. 'Is it death that comes upon you in your prime? Have the critics killed you at last?'

'More likely he's been eating lobster again,' put in his companion, a dapper fellow in evening dress. 'I hope he has,' he added vindictively, 'and that it kills him. I know he has the Rose Pearl, and, despite old friendship and all that, he treats me like any other bird from a paper — to use his own expression — and does me out of quite a comfortable little 'beat'.'

'Poor old Billy Wilson,' chuckled Frayne, 'wanted a scoop, and he couldn't get it! Well, I'm going to give it to you tonight, Billy, more even than you expected.

'But first I must be the perfect host. You both know Malcolm here, our tame sensationalist, but you must meet Crane: Mr. Wilson, Mr. Harley — Mr. Lionel Crane. This pair have been opponents of Malcolm's and mine for years. We play bridge here every alternate night. Harley looks glum, because a critic once told him that he might have been the greatest tragedian of all time, if it wasn't for his face, so he has spent years cultivating a sad and doleful air; Wilson is a public nuisance attached to some newspaper or other.'

'And Walle Frayne has the longest tongue in London,' added Wilson. 'We only put up with him because of his cellar. Now, what about this story of yours, Walle? Have you the Rose Pearl?'

Frayne smiled on the gathering; then without a word left the room by the door behind him.

'What — ' began Wilson; but Frayne returned before he could say more. Still in silence the actor held out his hand to his guests.

The room was in darkness save for the

one half-watt bulb, suspended in an ornate Eastern lamp over their heads. The light shone directly on to the pearl in Frayne's hand.

'By Jove, what a beauty!' exclaimed Wilson.

'Superb!'

'Turns mine into a mere bauble!'

'Here! What on earth — '

'Close your hand, Frayne! Quick!'

It was Lionel Crane's voice that rang out last. With terrifying suddenness the light over their heads had been extinguished, plunging the room into instant darkness. Even as he shouted Crane sprang in the direction in which his quick eyes had noticed the switch. He cannoned into another figure, which clutched at him wildly, and the two went down together in a struggling heap.

'I've got him!' shouted a voice from across the room. Crane and his assailant ceased struggling, and listened. Across the room was the sound of heavy bodies in violent combat.

Then, as suddenly as it had been extinguished, the light went up again. By the switch stood Wilson, the newspaper man; by the fireplace Frayne and Harley crouched on the floor and looked sheepishly at one another; Crane's strong hand still gripped Malcolm Page.

Harley laughed suddenly, a bitter laugh with no mirth in it. Crane's shrewd eyes narrowed. There was one peculiar fact about the men in the room. Each one of them was tall and slim. Just an odd coincidence; but by that same odd coincidence any one of these men might have been the Stealer.

'The pearl?' called Wilson. 'You've got it all right, Walle?'

The actor shrugged his shoulders.

'Gone, of course!' he replied bitterly. 'I had no chance to close my hand. The moment that the light went out my hand was knocked, and the pearl was removed. When I think of all my precautions — '

'You are sure,' questioned Crane, rising to his feet, 'that your hand was knocked almost simultaneously with the extinguishing of the light? There was no time, for instance, for an agile man to reach you after turning down the light switch.'

Frayne looked across to the door, by which the electric light switch was placed.

'Impossible!' he declared. 'It is a good ten paces to that switch, and there was not time for a man to take more than two.'

Crane looked at the others.

'I am afraid, gentlemen,' he said, 'that we will all have to submit to being searched.'

Wilson shrugged his shoulders.

'I'm game,' he replied; 'but it seems rather a waste of time. There was ample time for the criminal — supposing he is one of ourselves, which is rather laughable — to hide the pearl ten times over, while you people were grovelling about on the floor.'

'And you?' put in Page viciously. 'What were you doing?'

'Trying to find the light switch. I became muddled in the sudden darkness and searched along the wrong wall. But I should like to know what you mean by that question, Page?'

Crane laughed suddenly.

'We are not going to do much by

bickering amongst ourselves,' he pointed out with a great air of cheerfulness. 'I suggest that we line up and let Frayne search each of us in turn. Frayne, being the legitimate owner of the Rose Pearl, is hardly likely to have robbed himself.' The detective laughed again, and the others forced themselves to echo it.

With evident distaste for the task, Frayne obeyed Crane's instructions and searched each of his friends.

'Will you send for your man, Frayne?' asked Crane, 'while I 'phone Scotland Yard.'

'We don't want the police in,' protested Page. 'It will make us all look such fools; be in the papers, and all that.'

'It will be in the papers all right,' interrupted Wilson. 'You don't think I am going to miss a scoop like this, do you?'

'Use your own judgment about the police, Crane,' said Frayne. 'I don't want a terrific fuss, of course, in case — ' He looked oddly at the other men. 'Well, look here, let's be frank before Crane speaks to Scotland Yard. I am going to be absolutely blunt. Did one of you chaps work this

— as a practical joke, we'll say? You must remember that this will have serious consequences, and has already gone beyond a joke.'

He smiled encouragingly.

'We'll do what I have read of being done,' he decided. 'I am going to put this small table in the middle of the room. On the table is a small ash-bowl. Let's play the game, you fellows. While I stand at the light switch and keep the room in darkness for three minutes, I want the joke to end. Then we'll all toddle off home. What do you say, Crane?'

'An idea worth trying,' replied the detective. 'If it is a practical joke, I agree with you that it ought to end now. I agree to your terms.'

The others also signified their agreement.

'I hope that, whoever the funny idiot is, he will play up,' grumbled Wilson.

Frayne extinguished the light, and Crane, listening attentively, could hear the heavy breathing of those around him. Page gave his irritating little cough, and someone shuffled his feet.

'You know, I think this is rather a farce — ' began Harley suddenly; then the light blazed out again.

Crane's quick eye noted that each one of the men had shifted his position slightly.

Frayne advanced to the ash-bowl and took out of it a visiting card. On the one side was printed; 'Colonel Georges Duprez.'

'This was in the tray on my desk, where I keep the cards of all those who call on me,' muttered the actor. Absentmindedly, he turned the card over. Without a word, he handed it to Crane, and the detective read, in straggling, uneven capitals, that had evidently been freshly written in the dark:

'I WIN, CRANE. — P.S.'

'That door!' cried Wilson. 'It was shut when Frayne put the light out. I noticed especially!'

All turned.

The door leading into the hall was wide open.

7

The intruder

Crane dashed into the hall, followed closely by the others, but there was no sign of an intruder.

'You are sure that it was shut?' Page asked Wilson.

'I noticed it myself,' put in Crane.

'But Frayne was there — '

'I stood to one side by the switch,' replied the actor. 'It is just possible that someone may have passed me.'

Crane bent down by the door. When he rose to his feet the detective was examining the tips of his index finger.

'Oil,' he said laconically. 'The hinges have been carefully oiled recently. We can take it for certain that someone entered while the room was in darkness; the same person who reached a hand in and turned the lights off on the previous occasion.'

He turned to Frayne.

'Will you call your man at once, please?' he asked.

They all returned into Frayne's study, and the actor pressed the bell.

'How long have you had Pearson?' Crane asked, while they waited.

'Close on seven years,' was the reply.

'Who did you get him from?'

'He wasn't a professional valet,' confessed Frayne. 'I don't know what he had been, except that he told me that he had been to gaol on more than one occasion. You may well look surprised, but he used to be a criminal. He saved my life one evening, when I slipped in the road, and would have gone down under a bus. Pearson pulled me clear, and got laid out himself. I went to see him in hospital. The poor fellow was broke to the wide — absolutely down and out. For some reason that I could not quite gather, he was afraid to return to his trade of cracksman, and had been trying in vain to earn an honest penny.

'I told him that I would give him a chance. Of course, I watched him very closely at first, but he has been scrupulously honest with me, and, despite everything, I would trust him with my last penny.'

'He seems to be a long time in answering that bell,' interrupted Wilson, the journalist.

'I should like to say, Mr. Crane,' Harley said suddenly, 'that I have tried for some time to persuade Frayne to pass Pearson on to me. He has developed into one of the best servants in London. I have spoken with him frequently. The man is ludicrously grateful to Frayne for his chance, and has told me that nothing would drive him back to the hole-in-a-corner existence that he was living before. It has always struck me when he speaks of his former life that he has a powerful enemy, who makes it impossible for him to go back. I like Pearson, and will also vouch for him.'

'Once a crook, always a crook,' declaimed Page pompously.

Frayne returned while the two were arguing over Pearson's merits and demerits.

'He's not in the house,' he exclaimed.

'I've been to his room. All his kit is there, but of the man himself there is no sign.'

'I told you so!' cried Page. 'He has gone to take the Rose pearl to his master, the Phantom Stealer.'

'He might have gone for a chat with one of the other servants in the building,' suggested Harley. 'What do you think, Mr. Crane?'

The detective shrugged his shoulders.

'It is certainly strange for Pearson to be missing just at this moment,' he said. 'Of course, there may be a perfectly reasonable explanation as you suggest, Mr. Harley. We had better continue our investigations in other directions. If Pearson does not return in half an hour's time, we can take it for granted that his absence has something to do with the theft of the pearl.

'Now, while waiting for the police, who should be here shortly, I would like you all to sit by the fireplace, and remain in that part of the room, so that I can make a few investigations on my own. I don't like to have to say it, but I must point out to you that, under the circumstances, you must all consider yourselves under suspicion.'

Crane's laugh did much to relieve the words of some of their sting, but the three men eyed one another doubtfully, and sat in stiff silence.

Crane led Frayne to the far end of the room, and the two stood by the window, speaking in whispers.

'Tell me not only what you know yourself, but what you have heard of them,' explained the detective. 'It is for the best, Frayne. It will aid me to clear up this matter, and remove the uncomfortable atmosphere of suspicion.'

'It seems so absurd having to suspect one's friends,' grumbled the actor. 'Why, we've played bridge together in this flat for over a year.'

'Yes; but do you know anything about them beyond their small talk around the bridge table? Take Page. Where did you meet him?'

'Harley introduced him to me. He approached Harley through some mutual friend a long time ago because he had written a play, which he offered to Harley.

Harley took it. You may remember what a thundering success 'The Black Gun' was last year. That was Page's.

'Of course, it is absurd suspecting Page,' he added. 'More absurd the more I think of it. Why, the man is famous! Everyone knows him. You can't inquire into the pedigree of every man you meet. Besides, everyone knows about Page. He was a doctor until he made a success with his first book, and chucked doctoring to write others.'

Crane nodded. He had heard Page's history before, and knew that what Frayne was telling him was the truth. Page had had a small East End practice, to run which he had been hard put to it to make ends meet. He had written a book — a sensational crime story centring around the part of London which he knew so well. His book had been a tremendous success, and he had followed it up with others, equally successful, giving up his practice to devote his whole time to his new profession.

'What about Harley?' he asked.

'The son of famous old Bob Harley. Educated at Eton and Oxford. President of the O.U.D.S., which showed that he had inherited his father's talent, so the decision to make him a lawyer fell through, and he followed in old Bob's footsteps.'

'Wilson?'

The actor shrugged his shoulders.

'Billy Wilson was one of the first pals that I made in London twelve years ago. We have done most of our struggling together. I know him better than the other two. His father was a country parson. Billy shied at the Church, and had some stiff years breaking into journalism. I'll vouch for him. He wouldn't do a mean thing; and, above all, not one calculated to hurt me.'

As tactfully as possible, Crane cross-examined Frayne about his friends. He went deeper than their life-stories, and persuaded the actor to tell him all that he knew concerning their habits; the type of people that they mixed with; their tastes — what they smoked and drank, in particular.

'Cigarettes are Wilson's failing,' declared Frayne. 'Harley is given to an occasional cigar, but affects a pipe as part of his self-advertisement scheme. It is unusual to have an actor marching about London with a pipe shaped like a Turk's head. Page smokes very little; only cigarettes. I have never seen him with anything else. Drinks? Well, we'll all drink anything good. Brandy? An occasional liqueur. No, certainly, none of them drinks brandy as a habit.'

'Your half-hour is up, Crane,' called Wilson suddenly, 'and there is no evidence of Pearson having returned.'

At the same moment the doorbell rang, and Frayne admitted Detective-Inspector Herrick of Scotland Yard.

'I came alone, Crane,' he said, on entering, 'as you told me to, but I've got men outside the building. I was a long time in getting across here, because every possible thing happened to delay me.'

He looked curiously around the little group, and smiled at Wilson.

'What have you been doing this time?' he asked the newspaperman, who grinned back, and shook his head.

'Nothing. It's your friend the Phantom Stealer this time.'

At the name, the Scotland Yard man started excitedly.

'You were too late, Crane,' he cried, turning to the detective.

'In a way I was, and in a way I wasn't,' Crane replied. 'The pearl was safe when I got here. It was stolen while I was in the room; while I was looking at it, in fact.'

In a few brief words he gave Herrick an account of what had happened; the inspector's sharp eyes studying each of Walle Frayne's guests as he listened.

'There are two possibilities,' concluded Crane. 'Either the Stealer was hidden in this room, and snatched the pearl the moment that the light was extinguished, or — ' He shrugged his shoulders. 'In either case, there must have been an accomplice at the door, and events seem to point to it being Pearson, Mr. Frayne's manservant.'

'Pearson,' said Herrick, his eyes lighting up; 'of course, it's a common enough name, but there used to be a crook of that name. A fellow who disappeared some time ago. We came on to his name only this afternoon. I was going through all records of Gaudriol, and, when the Frenchman went to gaol, he accused Pearson of having sold him. It surprised everyone for Pearson had seldom worked with Gaudriol, as far as I could gather. Pearson disappeared within a couple of weeks of the trial, and has never been spotted since.'

'That will be our man,' decided Crane. 'I know now why his face was familiar to me.' The detective took a slip of paper from his pocket, and gave it a quick glance before returning it.

'I knew, of course,' confessed Frayne, 'that Pearson had been a crook, but I could have — in fact, I still am prepared to vouch for his honesty while he has been with me. The fellow has been most punctilious about all money matters, and I am sure was fond of me. I very much doubt whether he would willingly have robbed me of a possession which he knew that I prized so keenly.'

'I also am a great believer in Pearson,' put in Harley.

'Mr. Frayne used the word 'willingly',' Wilson pointed out. 'It is possible that this man, the Phantom Stealer, knew Pearson for what he had been, and forced him to aid in this robbery by threats of exposure.'

'That is possible,' assented Crane; 'but there is no sense in idly theorising. The next move will be to examine Pearson's room. There may be a clue there, which will take us a step further. If you do not mind showing us to the room, Frayne.'

The actor had provided well for his servant, for Pearson proved to have occupied an airy room at the other end of the flat. It had been comfortably furnished as a bed-sitting room. Pearson had evidently been proud of his quarters, for the room was scrupulously neat and clean, and the furniture shone with polish. A complete 'Self-Educator' in the bookcase, and sundry volumes on diverse subjects, showed how the ex-crook had improved the shining hour.

Crane opened the wardrobe, and

looked carefully at the neat clothes on their hangers. From there he studied the dressing table, and pulled a trunk and two suitcases from under the bed.

'He has gone without overcoat or hat,' he pointed out, 'and he has made no attempt to pack anything. That seems to do away with any idea of this being an organised raid, made with his assistance. It looks as though he discovered what had happened, and fled in a panic for fear that blame — '

The detective was in direct line with the door as he spoke. With a sudden bound he crossed the room and dashed into the narrow passage.

'After him, Herrick!' he shouted. 'He has just nipped down this way. I saw the dark figure.'

The Scotland Yard detective flung himself out of the door and lumbered after Crane, with Frayne and his friends close behind him. Herrick's voice rose over the sound of running feet, as he called to his men to stop anyone leaving the house. Ahead for a moment the pursuers caught a glimpse of a dark figure speeding across the hall. For a moment the man fumbled with the lock, jerked open the door, and slammed it behind him. He was only just ahead of Crane, who had to jerk his hand back to keep it from being jammed in the door.

There was a shout from outside.

'Got 'im, sir!'

Hurrying out, Crane found the fugitive in the massive grasp of one of the policemen that Herrick had brought with him. He strode forward, and flashed his torch into the white, scared face.

The man was Paul Gaudriol.

8

Gaudriol explains

'What are you doing here, Gaudriol?'

They had removed the ex-convict into Frayne's study, and a sorry-looking individual he was, crouching in an armchair. On each side of him stood a plainclothes man, while Herrick glowered at him from the fireplace. Frayne and his friends eyed the abject figure curiously.

Gaudriol's suit was torn, and he had much dirt and mould all over him. It was evident that he had been hiding for some time in the garden, while the tears in his suit and a scraped arm testified to his having climbed the wall, which was high and spiked at the top.

'I have done no wrong, Mr. Crane,' he pleaded. 'If I might only speak to you alone!'

Herrick grunted, but Crane led him

aside and, after a few moments' conversation, the Scotland Yard man called to his assistants and withdrew into the hall.

'If you gentlemen don't mind going with them,' suggested Crane.

'Well?' he asked Gaudriol, when they were alone. 'When you left me, it was to go to a lodging-house and lie low. How comes it that you are discovered here in this condition?'

Crane's face was stern and uncompromising. He had trusted Gaudriol, and breach of faith was a deadly crime in Crane' estimation.

'I was going, as I told you,' explained the other; 'but soon after I left your house, I saw Pearson — he used to work with me. I was behind him on a bus, and he did not recognise me.'

'Pearson? That is the man who has been working here for Mr. Frayne?'

'Yes, and the man who lied about me at the trial. He said that he would be revenged on me for not passing the pearl to him when I was caught.

'I remembered what you had said about the possibility of one of my former associates having murdered my wife. It seemed Fate that I should run into Pearson so soon after — I am a great believer in Fate — so I decided to follow Pearson.'

Crane's eyes gleamed with suppressed excitement.

'Where did he go? Did he come straight here?'

'No, he went to a house out Shepherd's Bush way first. I have written the full address out here. He was in there for over an hour. I began to fear that he had slipped out by the back entrance.

'When he came out he was very upset.'

Crane stopped the Frenchman.

'What exactly do you mean by 'very upset'?' he asked.

Gaudriol looked doubtfully at the detective.

'It is hard to explain,' he confessed, 'but I saw him full face for a moment, as he passed right close to where I was concealed. His face was very pale, and — well, I could swear that there were tears in his eyes.'

'Tears of rage?' suggested the detective.

The Frenchman shrugged his shoulders.

'I don't think so. I should be inclined to think that something had happened to Pearson in that house to move him very deeply. He walked for some way like a man in a dream. He walked into people and slipped twice on the edge of the pavement. Eventually, he pulled himself together and went to an Underground station and came straight here.

'Once again I hid myself in the garden and waited. I saw you arrive. I looked into the window of a room in which there was a light, and saw you and the four others standing together in the middle of the room. I saw more than that. I saw the door open and a hand reach for the light switch. When the light was extinguished I dropped to the ground again.'

'Why?'

'Because I knew the hand. It had always been a foible of Pearson's to wear a heavy signet-ring, and I recognised the ring on his finger.'

Crane nodded.

'I had suspected that the man who put

out the light was Pearson,' he said. 'Did you see anything else, Gaudriol?'

The ex-convict shook his head.

'I waited by the front door for some time; then I tried the window of one of the darkened rooms, and got inside. I hid, and heard you talking. I discovered that a pearl had been stolen, and, later, that Pearson had disappeared. I was following you to see what was discovered in Pearson's room when you came after me. I ran outside straight into the men there. That is all.'

Crane was silent for a while, studying Gaudriol with his sharp eyes. He was a keen judge of men, and something told him that the Frenchman's tale was the truth; but, Gaudriol was tall and thin, and in every respect fitted in with the character of the Stealer. Against that could be set the fact that Gaudriol had been in prison for many years, during which time the Stealer had been operating, but Crane never overlooked the most remote of possibilities. He had been a witness only recently at an inquiry into a prison scandal, at which it was proved beyond doubt that an influential prisoner with plenty of money behind him had been in the habit of leaving his prison at regular intervals to carry out a scheme of his. He had bribed royally, and the warders in his power would substitute another prisoner in the event of the missing man being sent for by the authorities.

There was just a chance that Gaudriol had been working according to the same plan. What better lair for a master-criminal to lie low in than a prison cell! After each coup he simply had to race back to Parkmoor, change into his convict garb, and relieve the man who had been acting for him in his absence.

The theory seemed too far-fetched for words, but it had proved correct once, so what was there to prevent it proving correct a second time?

The Stealer had proved himself possessed of reckless courage and unbounded cheek, so the idea of calling on Lionel Crane the moment that he was released from gaol would appeal to him. Crane considered the possibility from all sides, but there was one insurmountable item — the murder of Madeleine Gaudriol. If it had indeed been the Stealer who was after the Andapore Pearl, then the Stealer could not be Gaudriol.

On the other hand, the Stealer might have been visiting his wife, and some traitor in the Underworld warned the police in the hope that he would be captured. But the marks on the woman's neck!

Crane remembered also Gaudriol's perturbation when he failed to find Madeleine waiting for him at the prison gates, also when he came out from the Devon Hotel.

He shrugged his shoulders. There was no sense in idle theorising.

'Did you see anyone else around the building?' he asked.

Gaudriol shook his head.

'First one gentleman arrived,' he said. 'The one who was standing by the table there before you asked them to go out.'

Crane thought back, and realised that the Frenchman was referring to Malcolm Page.

'He seemed to be upset over something — very excited. He ran up the steps, leaving the door of his car open.

'Then you came; and shortly afterwards two others arrived together. They were talking about the pearl, and one of them — the younger of the two — said loudly as they passed me; 'I'll make him show it to me tonight, or my name's not Billy Wilson!' I heard him plainly. I was still around the house when Detective-Inspector Herrick hurried on to the scene; in fact, he brushed past me as close as you are now.'

'You did not see Pearson leave the house?'

'No, or I should not be here. I would have followed him. The first that I heard of his being missing was when you people spoke of it. That was why I risked entering the house. I will confess that I wanted to go through his kit in the hope of finding a clue to the murderer of my wife.'

Crane looked sharply at the cracksman.

'Do you think that Pearson murdered your wife?' he asked.

Gaudriol shrugged expressively.

'Who can say? I doubt it, because it does not agree with my idea of his character. He is a quiet chap. I was always surprised at his having turned crook at all. He is a very clever safe-breaker — there used to be no one with fingers quite as delicate as his. That was another strange thing about him. He must have been making pots of money, and yet he always dressed poorly, never had the price of a drink on him, and always seemed underfed. Pearson was a mystery to all of us. None knew where he lived, and he never appeared unless he had a job on.'

'What opinion did you form concerning him?'

'That he had been forced into crime against his will to pay off some big financial embarrassment; and that he was finding it all that he could do to meet the demands made upon him. He was always ready to take on any job that offered; but he made a point that violence was never to be used.'

Crane called Herrick and drew him aside to tell him what he had learnt from

Gaudriol, telling him also of the Frenchman's visit to Welbeck Street earlier in the day.

'I'll take him into custody for loitering around inhabited premises with the intent to commit a felony,' decided the inspector.

But Crane shook his head.

'No. Let him go, but keep him under the closest surveillance possible.'

'But — '

'Don't you see, Herrick, that he may lead us to our quarry. Even as he has followed Pearson, so will he go after all the men who may have had anything to do with his wife's death. In this way he may take us to our man. If he is the Stealer — which is just possible, though highly improbable — he is bound to make a slip soon.'

'I don't like letting him go,' grumbled the Scotland Yard man. 'He may slip through our fingers. He's a slippery customer.'

'He mustn't slip through your fingers. To make matters doubly certain, I am going to put Pollard on to him.'

Herrick nodded a doubtful assent.

'Have your own way, Crane. You seem to be able to pull these things off, but, frankly, I don't like it.'

Crane smiled his sudden smile.

'Neither do I, old chap; but in a case like this one has to take chances. So I want you to trust me this time.'

Frayne and his friends had come into the room, so the detective called them over, and Herrick asked them a few official questions. Then the Scotland Yard men were admitted and the room thoroughly searched.

'We might go through Pearson's things,' suggested Crane, 'while your men get busy.'

The ex-crook proved to have an extensive wardrobe of good clothes.

'I bought him the kit,' explained Frayne. 'The fellow really seemed to want to go straight and make up for his past, and I am one of those who believe a great deal in a man's personal appearance. Dress a man well and give him a comfortable room and some of the delicacies of life, and unless he has a definite criminal kink, he will have no desire to steal.'

'What did you pay him?' asked Crane.

'Eighty pounds a year, and, of course, all his keep. As I said, I also gave him most of his clothes.'

'Eighty? He should have been able to save something quite substantial out of that.'

Frayne grimaced.

'I am afraid that we had one or two discussions on that subject. He used to come frequently to me for advances, and when I asked him where the money went, he would look sheepish.'

'Gambling?' suggested Herrick. 'You can bet your boots that that is Pearson's trouble.'

'Did he ever have any visitors here?'

'Never.'

'What about his time off? What did he have?'

'He regularly had Wednesday evening and Sunday afternoon,' replied the actor. 'Of course, most evenings, after I had done with him, he would go out if he wanted to. Once or twice, he has asked me for a full day.'

'Have you any idea where he used to go?'

'None, I'm afraid. I ragged him once or twice about his 'best girl', but he merely ignored the hint, and closed up like a clam.'

'Has he mixed at all with any of the other servants in this building?'

'No. I suggested to him when I first took him on that he might care to make friends with Jimmy Dawes' man — a very good fellow — but Pearson pointed out that they would have nothing in common.'

Herrick took up the cross-examination while Crane carried on with his search of the room. With extreme care the detective turned out each of the pockets, feeling down into the linings and inspecting the very fluff that was disclosed. Pearson was too old a hand, however, to have left anything. The paucity of fluff went to show that he had been in the habit of cleaning his pockets regularly.

Crane turned his attention to the boxes. All were empty. At a nod from

Herrick, to whom he looked for permission, the famous detective took out a knife and slit the linings, probing the bottoms at the same time, Once more his search proved in vain.

Herrick concluded cross-examining Frayne, and proceeded to pull out all the drawers of the dressing table.

'Here's something!' he called suddenly, and held up a well-filled square envelope. 'Addressed very simply, what is more: 'To the Police'. I'll open this, Crane.'

All watched him with interest as he slit the envelope and disclosed a small brown pocket diary. With a tentative finger and thumb he began to turn the pages, while Crane looked over his shoulder.

'Seems to be his life history,' began Herrick.

For the second time that night the lights were extinguished with a sharp click. Crane reached forward to close his hand over the book before him, but someone else was before him. His strong fingers closed on to a sleeve, but it was dragged forcibly away. At the same moment, there was a distinct sound of a heavy blow, and Herrick cried out in pain.

Once again it was Wilson who relieved the darkness. He was standing by the switch when the lights went on again.

Stretched on the floor, with blood welling from a wound on his head, was Detective-Inspector Herrick.

9

Work for Pollard

Before anyone could reach him, Herrick groaned and stirred. Crane placed an arm under his shoulders and aided the Scotland Yard man to a chair. His assistants had come running from the other room at his shout.

'Did you pass anyone in the passage?' Crane asked them.

'No sir; no one at all,' was the reply.

'Guard the door, then. No one must go out of this room.'

Herrick revived slowly, and put his hands to his pounding head to which Crane applied the big sponge from the washstand.

'It must have been a blackjack,' Herrick muttered weakly.

'This must have been the weapon,' put in Harley's voice, and he held up a heavy reading lamp standard. 'It was on the

134

floor, and see, there is blood on it!'

'That diary!' whispered Herrick, holding out his hand — 'snatched away from me!'

Retained between his strong fingers was a torn fragment of paper, evidently the corner of a leaf from the missing book. Crane took it and looked at it curiously.

' . . . he has forced me to it all along . . . I have suspected — but now I know the truth I can unmask the Stealer . . . '

No other words were traceable on either side of the paper.

Once again each man in the room was subjected to a vigorous cross-examination, and Crane studied the lamp standard for any sign of fingerprints.

'No prints,' he reported. 'Our man either wore gloves or held this with the aid of a handkerchief — probably the latter. Of course, there are your prints here,' he said to Harley, 'but it was you who picked up the lamp.'

Herrick recovered sufficiently to take an active part in the inquiry, and Crane drew him to one side.

'We are up against a blank wall,' he decided. 'We can do nothing more here.'

'It must be one of these fellows,' grumbled Herrick, 'and yet we can take no proceedings against them. I've no grounds on which to make any arrest. I don't see how I could frame a charge.'

'We can do nothing like that,' decided Crane. 'We must let them all go.' He turned to the others. 'Gentlemen,' he said, 'I think that the best move is for us all to disperse for the night. There is nothing further that we can do. I should like all of you to come to my rooms in Welbeck Street at five o'clock tomorrow evening.'

'But, my pearl!' exclaimed Frayne.

'You can rest assured that I will do all in my power to recover it,' replied Crane. 'I can promise no more.'

'How much of this can I make public?' asked Wilson.

Crane was about to give unconditional permission to the newspaperman, but Frayne put in hurriedly:

'I would rather that this was kept out of the papers for a few days. I promised the countess that I would let no one know that I had the pearl before the end of the month. She is still waiting for her husband's permission to sell. He will give it all right, but he is in India. She has cabled him, and until she hears from him, the sale was to be kept secret. He is rather touchy about her doing things without his leave.'

Crane looked curiously at the actor, but said nothing. Wilson argued half-heartedly, but was overborne.

'All right,' he consented, 'I'll hang on for a while as a special favour to you, Frayne, but I want sole rights to the whole story when it can be made public.'

'I'll say goodnight, Gaudriol,' said Crane quietly. 'Remember to keep in touch with me. You are going to the address you gave me?'

'Yes, Mr. Crane, I shall go straight there.'

'Our luck seems dead out,' grumbled Herrick, as he and Lionel Crane travelled back to Welbeck Street together. 'Which-ever way we turn we seem to come up against a brick wall. Clue after clue comes into our hands, only to come to nothing. That diary, that I actually held in my hand, held the name of the Stealer, but he snatched it away before I could read it. We can take it for granted that he is either Harley, Page, or Wilson. And yet Page, you say, has been attacked by the Stealer himself.'

Crane shrugged his shoulders.

'It might be Gaudriol,' he replied.

'But Gaudriol was in gaol while the Stealer was operating!'

'I know; but you remember the Eckstein case. Eckstein worked from prison, coming out to put over his deals, and slipping back when things became hot.'

'That was an exceptional case, Crane, and prison discipline has been tightened up to prevent it happening again. I do not think it likely that Gaudriol can have duplicated Eckstein's methods. Besides, his wife would not have been reduced to pawning her belongings.'

Once again Crane shrugged non-committally.

'I had no chance to read anything in

that diary before the light went out,' he confessed. 'Did you make much of it, Herrick?'

'Nothing, beyond a sort of preface in which Pearson declared that the time had come to make a full confession. The sort of excitable stuff that one would expect a fellow to write under the circumstances. It's rotten luck, Crane, that we lost the chance to read the rest.'

Crane found Pollard waiting anxiously for him.

'I thought that you had got lost, Li,' explained the young man. 'Was just going to start a search. Now, I suppose we can go to bed in peace?'

'Not yet, Harry,' said Crane, and he recounted to Pollard the happenings of the night.

'Jove, Li, you seem to have stepped right on to it each time and yet missed it!' exclaimed the young man. 'But why not go to bed now? You need some rest.'

'I may try to snatch a slight doze, Harry, but I am afraid that I have work for you to do.'

Pollard's eyes gleamed.

'Good! I'm tired of hanging around here waiting for you to come in, Li. It's about time that I had something to do on this case. Just tell me what to do, and then watch me!'

'You are certainly going to have a job after your own heart tonight, Harry,' Crane declared with a smile. 'You are going to have to disguise yourself, and I know that nothing makes you happier than that.'

Crane told Pollard what he was to do, and the young man hurried gleefully from the room. Crane lowered himself into a comfortable chair and closed his eyes, but he was not sleeping, merely reviewing the factors in the extraordinary case that he was working on. Item by item, he studied all that had happened since the beginning, and pored over the few details that he had discovered. He was reviewing each of the men connected with the case, when there was a knock at the door and a seedy-looking individual entered.

The newcomer was dressed atrociously in what appeared to be cast-offs collected from a dozen different wardrobes, beginning with a rusty bowler hat and ending off with a pair of very ancient tennis shoes. His rubicund countenance was adorned with a weedy black moustache, and it was patent that he had not cut himself while shaving.

'You must tone down your colour a bit, Harry,' criticised Crane. 'The moustache is good.'

'I put it on hair by hair, Li,' replied Pollard, pleased with the knowledge that praise from Crane meant a good deal. 'I thought that I would limp — like this — as though I had done a great deal of tramping, and cultivate a plaintive whine: 'Life's bin 'ard on me, it 'as' — sort of thing.'

Crane assented.

'You must get near to Gaudriol, and in some way or other let slip something about having worked for the Stealer. I leave it to you. Gaudriol will go out of his way to cultivate your acquaintance then.'

After Pollard had shuffled out of the back door, Crane returned to his room and his armchair. Before long little was visible through a cloud of smoke.

In a quiet, methodical manner he reviewed all that had passed in the last twenty-four hours, and sorted out the channels down which inquiries might be made, and the clues that had come to his hand. He conjured up the scene in the bedroom at the Devon Hotel, when the body of Madeleine Gaudriol was discovered, and took up each of the points that might be of importance, viewing them in conjunction with the knowledge that the woman had died of poisoning.

The chain that had been around her neck was out of the ordinary, and might have been of use in establishing her true identity; but it was no longer required for that purpose. Still, it had left a very distinct mark on her neck, and would have made an impression on the hand of the man who dragged at it. Crane's eyes narrowed, and he puffed more furiously than ever at his pipe.

He rose to his feet after a while, and went into his laboratory. Here he took a small seed envelope from his pocket-case and extracted the paring of fingernail that he had collected from the body. For some length of time he was busy with a microscope. There were four short lengths of coarse light hair disclosed. He sorted these out, and, placing each in a separate test tube, proceeded to test the reactions of certain agents upon them.

He nodded with quiet satisfaction at the result of each test, and then cleaned his apparatus and placed the labelled tubes in a stand.

Once again he returned to his arm-chair. He turned his attention now to the attack on Malcolm Page, considering first the author's story of the attack made upon him in his study. He switched his mind back to the marks under the skylight, and the distinct track of small wheels from the library door. Why had Page lied in saying that the steps had never been brought into the study before?

Then the traces left by the Stealer were too obvious. Crane had had too great an experience of false trails to be taken in by so childish an attempt. Then again, he had examined the rainwater pipe, up which the man with a beard was supposed to have climbed. The smuts on it were undisturbed. No man had climbed that pipe, of this the detective was certain. On the roof was a set of well-defined prints leading from the top of the pipe to the skylight, but Crane's sharp eyes had not missed the carefully-obliterated trail which had originally led the other way. The fingerprints on the sill were mere smudges made with a pair of rubber gloves on to which rough prints had been stamped. On this point also Crane held no doubts.

Had Page lied all along, he wondered; or had the Stealer entered by some other way and left the false trail to confuse Crane?

Page had demanded police protection, but the Stealer had the impudence to make just such a move; and again, Page had been with Frayne when the Rose Pearl disappeared.

Crane filled a fresh pipe and removed the incidents at Malcolm Page's flat from his mind for the time being. He turned his attention to the finding of the body of Detective-Sergeant Greene. Greene must have been murdered while Crane was in his study with Gaudriol. That seemed to clear the Frenchman. The murder of the detective was one of the most callously brutal crimes that Crane had come across. It would have been as simple to stun the detective and leave him bound in the kitchen of the house. The murder was unnecessary. The Stealer must realise also that by this crime he had set his trackers after him with still stronger purpose.

'It must have been a fit of ungovernable rage,' Crane told himself. 'This was no premeditated crime. He suddenly realised that Greene had tracked him to his lair, and, without considering the consequences, he struck. He must have regretted the step when it was too late. This points to the Stealer being of an excitable temperament, and given to bursts of almost insane temper.'

Next Crane considered what he had discovered in the Stealer's lair. Herrick was following up the clues of the camp bed and the other furniture. There remained the car. Crane decided to interview the cook who had spoken to

Herrick and himself. She had appeared to be an intelligent woman, and would have noticed if a car had been in the habit of standing by Number Fourteen. He would pay a visit to the street in which Number Fourteen stood early the next morning.

From Number Fourteen the detective's mind took him to Frayne's flat. His suspicions had been aroused on finding Page there, but the author's visit was very simply explained. He had come for the double purpose of playing his customary game of bridge and to recount his adventure with the Stealer. Frayne's declaration that he hoped the Stealer would attack him fitted in with the actor's bombastic character. Then had arrived Wilson and Harley.

Crane drew a sheet of paper and a pencil towards him and roughly sketched the three men — Page, Wilson and Harley. He went over every word of their conversation that his trained memory had retained; seeking everywhere for a slip — some phrase which did not fit in with their characters.

He made a sketch map of the study and

marked the position of each man before the light was extinguished for the first time.

Then he considered Pearson. He turned up his Rogues' Gallery and studied the photographs of the crooks that were in it; and at the same time reviewing what he had discovered of the man's history and character.

He took from his pocket the visiting card on which the Stealer had written his impudent message. There was no doubt but that the letters had been hurriedly printed in the dark. He compared them with the previous note that he had received on the occasion of the attack on Page. His brow clouded. Allowing for everything, it was obvious to a student of handwriting that the two could not have been written by the same man. The pressure on the pen was entirely different.

He drew from his pocket-case the scrap from Pearson's diary; and the cloud on his forehead became blacker. The writing on the second note from the Stealer — the one that had been found in

Frayne's flat — bore a distinct resemblance to that in the diary. Crane made a few simple comparisons and tests, and before long was convinced. If Pearson had written the diary then Pearson had written on the back of the visiting card.

But Pearson had not written the other note signed 'The Phantom Stealer'. Could there be two Stealers?

Crane continued with a consideration of Pearson's character, and turned over in his mind what Gaudriol had said concerning him. He read the address in Ewe Road, Shepherd's Bush, at which Pearson had called when Gaudriol was trailing him, and made a note to call there on the morrow. At that address he might at least discover the reason for Pearson's greed for money, which he never spent on himself.

The detective suddenly rose to his feet, took off his dressing gown and collected a hat.

'There's no time like the present,' he decided. 'As Pollard would put it, I am going to work on a hunch.'

He walked over to the garage for the

Grey Panther, but changed his mind at the door, and hailed a taxi.

'Eighty-two, Ewe Road, Shepherd's Bush,' he instructed the driver. 'Do you know the road?'

'Yes, sir. Which it ain't many drivers as would, but me sister lives there,' was the reply.

Crane dismissed his taxi some distance from the house that he was heading for and finished his journey on foot. Number 82 proved to be one of a row of neat houses, with freshly painted railings, and every indication of belonging to better class families. The light shone pleasantly through a gay green blind in the window by the door of 82. Crane raised the highly-polished knocker and rapped lightly.

The door opened almost immediately, and a man's white, drawn face peered at the detective.

'I — I — kind of hoped that you would follow me here, Mr. Crane,' muttered Pearson. 'Will you come in?'

10

Father and son

The room that Pearson led Crane into proved to be one of the most cosy little libraries that he had ever seen. It was evident that much love and care had been spent on its furnishing. The walls were lined with bookshelves and glass-doored cabinets. Across one corner was a spinet that made Crane open his eyes, for the detective knew a great deal about old furniture, and this piece was a gem. A tallboy also attracted his notice, and he marvelled at the price that must have been paid for it. In the cabinets were other choice pieces of art that would have sent more than one collector crazy.

On the walls were only four pictures — high up, over the books — but each one was the work of a master, and worth a fabulous sum. Crane recognised the Corot that had been bought by a mysterious purchaser some time before, and remembered that the price had been well-nigh a record.

Drawn up close to a cheery fire was a long invalid-chair, in which reclined a very ancient man. Crane realised that disease as well as age had lined the waxen face, and taken all the flesh from the nervous artistic fingers. The suspicious, darting eyes were also clouded, and showed that the brain behind them was not unimpaired.

'This is my father, Mr. Crane,' explained Pearson nervously. 'He has been an invalid for many years. Father — ' he shouted, 'this is Mr. Lionel Crane, the private detective.'

The old man was evidently deaf, for he cupped his ear and muttered a querulous: 'Eh?'

Pearson patiently repeated the introduction, and the old man offered a skinny hand, which Crane shook, smiling quietly into the dim eyes. Crane, like many men of action, had a soft corner in his heart for old people, and Pearson's father made a splendid picture of dignified old age with his wisps of white hair and placid, child-like eyes.

'What do you want with a detective?' he asked his son. 'Has he come about my watch?'

Pearson smiled affectionately on the old man.

'I'll tell him about your watch,' he promised.

'No, you won't. I'll tell him myself. My watch has gone. I have had it for — how long, Harry — ? Forty years; and now it has gone. I went to wind it this morning, and it was not on my dressing table. I can't move by myself, you know, Mr. Crane,' he explained, ' — so Harry always puts my watch on the dressing table by my bed, so that I can wind it as soon as I wake. He's a good son is Harry.'

He smiled at the confused Pearson, who paled and looked beseechingly at Crane.

'Are you sure that Harry did not forget the watch for once?' the detective asked. 'Perhaps he was busy?'

'He always is busy. These days he never seems to be here at all. I don't know why he doesn't live here with me always,' grumbled Pearson's father. 'I hate Gummidge. Clumsy, that's what she is; and she forgets things. Made my pudding too hot today, that's what she did. Do you hear that, Harry. Burnt me, she did!'

'Mrs. Gummidge looks after him while I am away,' explained Pearson. 'But we will go into the next room to talk, Mr. Crane. We have to talk business, father.'

'Business — always business!' snorted the old man. 'And Mr. Crane hasn't seen my collection. I was famous as a collector before my stroke,' he boasted, 'but with Harry's help, I have excelled all my dreams. Look round this room — all mine!'

He insisted on Pearson wheeling him around the room, while he pointed out his treasures to Crane. The detective realised the extraordinary bond of affection between these two, and his sharp eyes noted the glances that Pearson gave at the photograph of a very beautiful woman in the dress of many years before.

'My wife, Mr. Crane,' said the old man as his chair stopped by the photograph.

'She died some years ago. Harry has looked after me since that, haven't you, boy?'

Pearson inclined his head.

'I promised her I would,' he said quietly.

'Looked after me well, too,' declared the old man. 'I was afraid that I would die — a poor old man in poverty. I lost my wife and my money both together, Mr. Crane, but I have not missed either. Harry seems to have an unlimited supply of money, and my wife, I know, is waiting for me.'

Pearson managed to persuade the garrulous old man to consent to being left in his favourite place by the fire. As he closed the door, and he and Crane were in the next room alone, he dropped limply into a chair. The mask of cheerfulness had slipped from his face, which was haggard and as white as death.

'You understand now, Mr. Crane,' he said simply.

The detective laid a sympathetic hand on the criminal's shoulder.

'I had an idea of something like this

before,' he confessed. 'It was the only possibility that fitted in with your actions. I will confess, however, that I expected it to be a woman.'

Pearson's eyes travelled to a replica of the photograph of his mother, which was in this room also, and Crane realised that there had always been but one woman in his life.

'You steal to keep him comfortable, Pearson?'

'Yes. And so that he can surround himself with the works of art that he loves. I could not make enough money in any other way. I know that I have been a fool, but it seemed so simple, and once I had started it was impossible to draw back. Besides, it was not to provide him with luxuries that I started. It was a matter of an operation — life and death! Only one man in London could pull him through, and his fee — the very least that he would make it — was five hundred guineas. It was an out of the ordinary operation, a difficult one. The surgeon risked failure, and wanted paying to take that risk. I had barely five hundred pence

155

at the time. So I took the first step. I have always had sensitive fingers. I discovered that I could turn them to good account with a little practice.' He shrugged his shoulders. 'I found that I could open any ordinary safe with comparative ease. It was not long before I discovered a market.

'I heard my fellow-cracksmen talking. They seemed to consider our job in the light of a profession. I also became blinded to the criminality of it, and began to enjoy surprising my father by my prodigality with money. As I have said, I was a fool! A criminal fool!'

'You worked for Gaudriol,' said Crane.

'Yes; but only once.'

'What did you mean by declaring at the trial that he had double-crossed you?'

'I have since discovered that I made an error. At the time of the trial I had not received the sum that was due to me for my work. It was paid to me afterwards by one of Gaudriol's agents. I am afraid that mixing with crooks had made me view things in their way. That was what made me say all that about revenge.'

'You also worked for others?'

'Yes.' Unhesitatingly Pearson gave Crane a list of the crimes that he had assisted at.

'On each occasion I got no share of the actual booty, but was paid a lump sum for my services, which was paid half in advance. If we pulled the show off, I got the other half. If we failed, I had something to go on with, anyway.'

'No one in the underworld knew of your place here?' asked Crane.

'No.'

'You kept a diary?'

'Yes. I am glad that you found it. You will know the truth now. I had suspected it all along, but this last episode has proved it.'

Crane leant forward and stared piercingly at the criminal.

'We did not learn the truth from your diary,' he said, 'because it was snatched from our hands. I want you to tell me what was written there. But, first, what were you doing with Walle Frayne? The story that you wished to turn over a new leaf is too ridiculous for consideration. You have this cosy home to retire to. I want the truth, remember, Pearson. What were you doing with Frayne?'

Pearson looked doubtfully into the detective's eyes.

'I think you know without my telling you — ' he began.

Then, from the next room, there was a shrill scream — a scream of unutterable agony. With one accord the detective and the criminal leapt for the door. Pearson reached it first and led the way into the next room. He let out a cry of horror, and sprang forward with outstretched hands.

Crane, also, after one look at the tragedy before them, dashed forward to aid the criminal in his struggle with death.

The invalid chair had fallen on to its side, and Pearson's father lay with his head in the grate, and his whole figure a blaze of flames. In reaching for something from the table, he must have tipped over his chair, and in falling become unconscious. Only after his clothing was well alight had the pain roused him sufficiently to give him the strength to scream.

Recklessly Pearson snatched the thin

figure from the floor and attempted to press out the flames by hugging it to him. Crane seized a blanket and flung it around the two of them, for already Pearson's own clothing was alight; but the criminal's frenzied efforts to save his father hindered Crane, and before long the flames were gaining a strong hold on both of the men.

Jumping in, Crane knocked Pearson out with a terrific uppercut and contrived to beat out the flames on the still body. One look at the father told him that he could do nothing there. He felt for Pearson's heart, and was horrified at the weakness of the movement.

Without wasting a fraction of a second the detective forced brandy from his flask between the man's lips. Then he ran from the room and brought a flour bin from the nearby kitchen, and all the clothes that he could find. He had already observed that more than one third of the skin seemed to have been destroyed, and that the shock was going to be difficult to combat.

Believing in simple remedies while

more elaborate ones were being prepared, the detective shook flour over the exposed burns until they were well covered, and, making Pearson as comfortable as possible, filled empty whisky bottles with hot water and placed them at the man's feet and to each side of him.

Once he had done all he could for the time being, Crane hurried to the 'phone. On the memo-tablet was a doctor's name and number, so the detective called the doctor who had evidently been attending old man Pearson.

Then he returned to Pearson. Inwardly he was fuming against the perverseness of Fate. Once more victory had been snatched away from him at the last moment.

He bent over Pearson, who was moaning, and was apparently bordering on consciousness. If the man could only speak before he died!

'Pearson!' Crane called quietly.

The man moaned, but no reply came from his scorched and twisted lips.

'What were you doing with Frayne?' Crane asked.

Pearson seemed to understand that, for his lips moved. Crane bent close, every nerve strained as he listened.

'What were you doing with Frayne?' he repeated doggedly.

When the doctor arrived, he shook his head over Pearson's body.

'The shock of his father dying would have killed him, anyway,' he told Crane. 'I have never known a son so devoted; and he had a weak heart, you know, so the shock would have been too much.'

★　★　★

A private hotel in Kensington may seem a strange place for a criminal to live, but the days of underground dens in Limehouse are disappearing with the growth of the new type of cracksman. The old lairs were fitting for the old 'tough', but a man like Gaudriol wanted something much better.

Mrs. Lamb offered select board-residence to retired Army officers, clergymen's widows and Colonials seeing the Old Country, also students, and any others who would come. But all had to be respectable. Mrs. Lamb possessed a colonel, who sat in the window, and all had to pass his eagle eye. He had been her star attraction for years.

Mrs. Lamb was more than pleased to receive Monsieur Jules Mecredi back again after so long an absence, and the reunion between him and the bluff colonel was reminiscent of Blucher and Wellington after Waterloo.

'By gad, sir! This is the best day since an occasion in Poranpore, when young Wilmott and I — by gad, we were lads in those days!' bellowed the colonel.

Monsieur Jules sighed sadly, for Mrs. Lamb had interrupted the colonel to ask after Madame Mecredi.

'Alas!' he murmured, and the pain in his eyes was real. 'She is dead!'

The colonel trumpeted into a large handkerchief, and Mrs. Lamb permitted a discreet tear to trickle to her cheek. Monsieur's wife had been not only beautiful, but kindness itself to all and sundry.

The Frenchman insisted on hurrying to his room. He did not want to speak of

Madame — his bereavement was too fresh. Once the door had closed after the voluble Mrs. Lamb, Gaudriol flung himself on his bed to think. His face was not pleasant in its grim lines, for he was considering again the murder of Madeleine.

Annie McTavish, Mrs. Lamb's chef, was a large, raw-boned, red-headed Scotswoman, with a chin like a battleship, eyes like gimlets, and a heart as soft as her exterior was grim. Early on the morning after the return to the fold of the affable Monsieur Jules, she opened her kitchen door to take a breath of air before attacking the breakfast eggs, which were awaiting her. Her steely eyes considered a pair of white tennis shoes, which poked out from a pile of empty cases in the corner of the area. Stepping lightly back into the kitchen, she seized a broom and sailed into the fray.

'Sleeping in my area, are ye, ye awfu' blaggard, ye!' she admonished the drowsy one, who scurried from his refuge and made a wild dive for the steps. But Annie was too swift for him, and a skilful thrust between the shins with the handle of the broom precipitated the seedy individual on to the crown of his already dilapidated bowler.

'Now,' she warned, standing over him belligerently, 'ye ken that I'm no allowing no nonsense. For what reason are ye sleeping in a respectable woman's area?'

Pollard collected his rather scattered wits, and commenced a plaintive story about having been a gentleman's valet and losing his job when his master died, and having been out of work ever since.

Throughout the recital the sharp eyes studied him, and the soft heart pitied him.

'When did you eat last?' she asked suddenly.

'Not for I don't know how long,' Pollard replied vaguely.

'Get up,' she commanded, 'and get yesel' into the kitchen!'

Nothing loth, Pollard hurried along before her, and, in a very short space of time, was seated at a table with a healthy repast before him. He was tucking in for all his worth, and contriving to give a very creditable display of a starving man tasting his first bit of food for some considerable time, when Mrs. Lamb arrived in the kitchen.

'Annie!'

Her face was a study of amazement and rage combined, and she gestured weakly at the shabby figure at her kitchen table. Annie drew herself up and launched an attack with her heaviest guns.

'Take my notice, mum,' she said bitterly. 'Ye'ill get anither body to cook for ye, na' doot. I'll be goin', for I couldna stay where the puir an' the ootcast are turned away empty. Sie a young man, an' ye would be turnin' him away to starve!'

'But, Annie — '

A new thought seemed to strike the cook.

'Mum, take a keek at this young man. Respectable. Clean. Wouldna he suit ye in buttons? Wouldna he be the makin' o' ye hoose? He would!'

Pollard had risen to his feet, and stood sheepishly by the table, fumbling with his hat. He decided that the time was ripe to come to Annie's assistance.

'I've been a gentleman's valet, madam,' he assured the agitated Mrs. Lamb. 'I would repay your kindness if you could give me a position. I know the work well, and would suit you.'

'He'd no be wanting muckle wages, mum,' rapped Annie with a fiery eye on Pollard, who shook his head strenuously.

'Just enough to keep body and soul together, madam,' he declared.

Annie won her battle, and Pollard entered into the employment of Mrs. Lamb as, to use his own term — 'general nuisance and bottle-washer'. His first duty, as impressed upon him by Mrs. Lamb, was to knock on doors number five and nine, and offer his services as valet — with Mrs. Lamb's compliments — to Colonel Bore-Talkington and Monsieur Jules Mecredi.

11

The poisoned milk

Crane and Herrick stood together in Pearson's house. The bodies of the two unfortunate men had been removed, and the two detectives had the house to themselves.

'Good stuff!' said Herrick, indicating the furniture. 'Cost some money. No wonder Pearson was always broke.'

They began an exhaustive search of each room. The hope lay in the possibility that Pearson had left some other clue behind him to the identity of the Stealer. It soon became apparent that Pearson had never expected this house of his to be raided, for plentiful evidence of all his crimes was soon forthcoming. Herrick whistled at some of the discoveries, which threw light on many unexplained mysteries that had been puzzling the police for some time. But the one thing that they were looking for was absent. There was no mention of the Stealer anywhere, and no explanation of his taking employment with Walle Frayne.

'I'll round up all the addresses first thing tomorrow — or, rather, this morning. I have a man calling on the big stores about that camp furniture also. You can leave all that to me, and I'll ring your chambers at any development.'

Crane stopped the Scotland Yard man as he was about to make his departure.

'We must not lose sight of the fact that we have two mysteries to solve, Herrick,' he reminded him. 'Could you let me have a full report of the analysis finding in the case of Madeleine Gaudriol? I want to study it. What was the poison?'

'Arsenic,' replied Herrick, reaching into a capacious pocket. 'Here's a summary of his evidence at the inquest.'

Crane took the document in question and seated himself in a chair in the library. The fire had destroyed the carpet around the grate, and had blistered the chimneypiece and some of the precious furniture; but it had spent itself on its human victims, and had done but little damage to the room.

The pathologist's report was brief, but full of interest.

'Death was caused by syncope, due to acute arsenical poisoning. I discovered no less than two grains of arsenic in the body. Other symptoms to point to the cause of death were the fatty degeneration of the heart, liver, and kidneys.'

Crane raised his eyebrows at the quantity of arsenic discovered, for he knew that a medicinal dose did not exceed one-sixteenth of a grain. In silence, he read on:

'The marks on the neck showed that pressure had been brought to bear, but not of a nature capable of causing death by itself. I am given to understand that Madame Bourchaud complained of feeling unwell soon after nine on the evening of her death and retired to bed. I am of opinion that a dose of arsenic, of not sufficient quantity to prove fatal, was taken by Madame Bourchaud in the course of the afternoon, but that after retiring to her room the least possible fatal dose was taken. Examination of the room has proved that madame was violently ill during this period: and there was an empty glass that had contained milk on the washstand. I have analysed the residue in this glass, and have discovered traces of arsenic therein.'

Appended to the pathologist's report was a sheet of paper on which Herrick, or one of his men, had made notes. Crane read these with interest.

'The lady was in the habit of having a glass of milk three times a day — at eleven in the morning, four in the afternoon, and when she went to bed. Was taken ill after four o'clock milk, but seemed to recover. Milk supplied by the Superb Dairy Company in sealed bottles. Delivered to M. B.'s room in bottle. Decanted by her. Bottle handled by dairyman, kitchen maid at

Devon Hotel, and chambermaid. Dairy-man been fifteen years with firm; kitchen maid and chambermaid under observation, and histories being sought. Unfinished portion of four o'clock milk given to cat. Cat sick. But poisoning not suspected as cat given to over-indulgence.'

★   ★   ★

Crane returned to Welbeck Street with two more calls on his list for the day's work — one to the Devon Hotel, and one to the Superb Dairy Company.

He found the manager of the Devon in a worse humour than usual, and it was some while before he could get a word in edgeways, for the little man seized the excellent opportunity to unload his troubles on one of the men whom he considered responsible for them.

'If you haf not come, there haf not been troubles!' he kept vociferating with much waving of the hands. 'Now my peoples leaf me. Other peoples vill not come. And the hotel, it go bang — phut!'

Crane managed to calm him in his

suave way, and asked to see first the chambermaid and then the kitchen maid.

The little man shrugged his shoulders resignedly.

'They vill leaf me now. Soon I haf no peoples and no servants.'

Nevertheless, he sent for the chambermaid.

'Minnie,' he said, when a comely, smiling girl entered, 'this shentlemans vants to talk to you.'

'If you don't mind leaving us,' said Crane and the irate little man bounced himself out of the room.

With both the servants Crane's method was the same. When each one entered, he was lolling back in his chair, staring dreamily at nothing in particular, but, when she approached close, he swung round suddenly and peered into her face.

'Why did you kill Madame Bourchaud?' he demanded sharply, the words coming out like the crack of a whip, and one finger pointing menacingly at the girl.

In the case of Minnie, the chambermaid, the result was an indignant declaration of innocence, and it took all the detective's tact to send her from the room pacified.

But with the kitchen maid he received his reward. She proved to be a thin, undersized creature — very young — with a pale face and a nervous trick of twisting her fingers together behind her back.

At Crane's brutal accusation, she burst into tears, and flopped on to the floor as though her legs were too weak to bear her weight. One look at the terrified face told the experienced eyes of Crane in what agony she had lived since the crime.

'I — I didn't kill her!' she sobbed.

'No,' rasped the detective, forcing himself to be cruel, 'but you helped. You allowed him to poison her milk.'

Again the girl let out a cry, and her sobbing increased in volume.

'I never thought — ' she wept. 'He said that it, would be all right. I never guessed, even when — it happened. It was last night — when I was in bed — that I — I guessed!'

Crane laid a sympathetic hand on her shoulder, and helped the sobbing girl to a chair. The time for harshness, he knew, was past, and in his quiet voice he set to work to comfort the girl and to draw her story from her. At the back of his mind he was rejoicing. He had not expected success at the first attempt. He was no great believer in third degree methods, but, in this instance, they had been his one chance, although it had hurt him to be forced to use them.

'Now,' he said quietly, when she had recovered somewhat, 'tell me all that happened.'

'Madame's milk had come, and then Frank came along, sir, an' 'e said as he was one bottle short for an old lady what would get 'im the sack if 'er milk was late. It was only ten o'clock, so there was 'eaps of time for 'im to fetch another bottle for madame, an' be back with it before eleven. So — so I gave 'im 'ers, an' 'e was back before 'alf-past with another bottle. I never thought I was doing wrong, sir! It — it was such a small thing to do for 'im!'

She fingered an ornate ring on the third finger of her left hand.

'He gave you that?' asked Crane.

'Yes, sir. We was engaged.'

She flushed as she said the words, and the tears rushed to her eyes again. Crane smiled kindly.

'Don't worry,' he reassured her. 'There'll be a better man one of these days. Tell me something about him — Frank?'

Slowly, the pitiful little story came out. She had met him at a cinema. They had started talking over an incident on the film. He was tall and dark, with a small moustache and an engaging smile. He seemed to have plenty of money, but he confessed to her that he was out of work.

He seemed interested in the work that she was doing, and, being somewhat lonely, she prattled a great deal concerning the Devon and the people in it. She could not remember having told about Madame Bourchaud's milk, but she confessed that she probably did.

One evening when they met, he told her that his troubles were over, as he had got a job with the Superb Dairy Company. The Devon was not on his circuit, so he would not have the joy of delivering milk into her hands, but, still, he would now be able to save up for the day when they might get married.

By this subterfuge, it had been a simple matter for him to get hold of Madame Bourchaud's milk before it went up to that lady's room.

'What about the second bottle in the evening?' asked Crane. 'Did he do the same again?'

'Yes,' she confessed tearfully; 'an' we didn't arf laugh over 'is forgetting.

'I never thought — even when she was took ill — an' — an' when she died. It didn't seem as it could be 'im! When the police saw me an' asked me about the milk, I never thought. It was last night, after 'e 'adn't been there to meet me, that — that it sort of came with a bang! I knew then! But I couldn't think what to do!'

Crane considered the girl thoughtfully.

'For now,' he told her, 'you must just keep quiet and say nothing to anyone. You have been very foolish in trusting a man that you knew so little about, with terrible results; but you have learnt your lesson, and will be more careful in future.'

'I will, sir! Oh, I will!'

'I want you to think very hard,' continued the detective, 'and try to tell me more about this man. What name did he give you?'

'Frank Epping, sir.'

'What sort of man was he?'

'Very gentlemanly, sir. He spoke proper. I — I was surprised that he liked me. I — I thought as I was lucky!'

'Did you notice anything special about him?'

'He was always dressy, sir. 'E wore a blue suit an' black shoes always, and a 'ard 'at. There was one thing, sir — 'e said it was the war 'ad done it — but 'e limped something awful! 'Is left leg, it was, sir.'

'Curly hair?' asked Crane, a moment later, after noting down the important point of the limp.

'No, sir. Straight 'air. 'E wore it long and artistic-like. 'E 'ad dark-brown eyes, sir.'

'Big hands?'

'Long 'ands, sir. And 'is feet made me

laugh; they was so small for such a big man, sir.'

After a few more questions, Crane dismissed the girl with the assurance that she was not to worry, and that she was to repeat to no one what she had just told him. Then he called a taxi and hastened to the address that Gaudriol had given to him. His next move was to see whether Gaudriol could recognise the man who had called himself Frank Epping from his description. If Gaudriol failed him, Crane could take the girl to Welbeck Street and let her look through his Rogues' Gallery, for he was certain that Frank Epping would have a place there. His method of working bore the stamp of the polished crook, and the detective had no doubt but that the murderer had indeed been a former associate of Gaudriol's seeking revenge.

He found Mrs. Lamb's boarding-house in a state of uproar. Annie, the chef, was in the hall giving notice at the full force of her powerful lungs, while Mrs. Lamb gave vent to a fit of hysterics in the somewhat reluctant arms of her colonel, who was attempting to shout Annie down with a variety of strange oaths reminiscent of India.

The detective introduced himself quietly into the uproar.

'The laddie canna ha' been a villin,' Annie was shouting. 'Monsieur Mecredi will ha' ganged oot an' taken the laddie along wi' him. Dinna fash yesel', mum! I canna worrk in a hoose wha' folks canna keep calm. I gie ye my notice, mum. I'll be ganging awa' to anither place.'

'Might I ask what the trouble is?' Crane asked during a lull. 'I am a detective.'

'Saints alive!' exclaimed Annie, and disappeared down to the basement. As she explained to the kitchen maid: 'You wouldna' ha' a body argie wi' a policeman! It's no reet!'

Mrs. Lamb recovered sufficiently to stand on her own feet, and the colonel, bowing stiffly, hobbled away.

'I came,' explained Crane, 'to see Monsieur Mecredi.'

At the name, Mrs. Lamb promptly burst into tears again.

'He's gone!' she sobbed. 'Disappeared!

I showed him to his room last night — very late it was. Then, this morning my cook — the woman who was here just now — insisted on my taking on a stray individual as a valet. I am certain that he was the cause of the trouble. At breakfast time, Monseiur Mecredi did not appear. When he stayed with me before, he was always most regular in his appearance at meals. I, myself, went to his room. He was not there. His bed had not been slept in.'

'And this individual whom you took on as a valet?' asked Crane, who guessed that this must have been Pollard and was anxious for the fellow's safety.

'He also has gone! Both of them have disappeared!'

12

At the Canton Cafe

Some moments passed between the instant when Pollard knocked on the door of Number Eight and the invitation to enter. He discovered that the Frenchman had not been to bed, but was seated at a table with a pencil and writing pad before him. The young man had to look twice before he could pierce the disguise and recognise Gaudriol. The cracksman had added a neat, dark moustache and side-whiskers, and had placed a gold shield over a centre tooth. These few changes, in conjunction with a pair of pince-nez on a broad black ribbon and a general accentuation of his French accent and manner, formed a most efficient disguise.

'What ees it?' he demanded. 'Me, I am busy, and I desire to not be worried. Ees it that I must write zee notice for the door

— 'Go away. I am busy!'?'

'Sorry, sir,' said Pollard, 'but I'm the valet, and the lady told me to come to you. Shall I put out a change of clothes, sir — ? You haven't unpacked yet — and I'll prepare a bath for you.'

The Frenchman frowned, then laughed.

'Madame is too good,' he declared. 'Another day, yes, I shall be too much pleased at your service, but, for now, I have zee work. I must finish, and then I must post heem.'

Pollard bowed politely and withdrew; but he contrived to busy himself on the landing and, when the door of Number 8 opened, to slip into a bathroom out of sight.

Gaudriol had his hat on when he came out, and his actions were furtive, for he looked carefully around before creeping downstairs. With Pollard after him he crossed the empty hall, and let himself out into the street. Here also he took great pains to keep out of sight from the windows of Mrs. Lamb's.

He entered the first available taxi, and drove in an easterly direction, with

Pollard aided by the darkness, following as close behind as he dared. By good fortune Pollard was also able to pick up a taxi, and the chase began.

Gaudriol took no precautions, but drove straight to the Canton Chop-suey in Water Causeway. Here he paid off his taxi, and entered with the casual manner of a habitué.

Pollard left his cab way down the road, and spent a few moments buying a cap and an old brown overcoat from a shopkeeper, who tactfully asked no questions. Changes of attire were apparently frequently bought over the counter and donned in this shop, and the owner had found it healthier to appear to treat the deals as a matter of course.

In a dark doorway he scrubbed off his moustache, with the assistance of coco-butter, which he had carried around in his pocket, and spread a good coating of grease and dirt over his face.

Then he also entered the Canton.

The restaurant was in the form of a long centre space littered with small marble-topped tables, off which opened small cubicles, each containing a table and four chairs. One paid no extra for the privacy of a cubicle, but one had to take one's chance of securing one. There was a counter at the far end, and behind it sat a slim half-caste in European clothes. He was totting up figures in a book when Pollard entered, and paid no attention to the young man as he made a tour of the place before selecting a table. Many of his customers had their preferences, and there was nothing out of the ordinary in the fellow's actions. The man was not paid to be suspicious.

The tables in the centre space were all vacant, and only two of the cubicles had occupants. In one was quite a well-dressed girl, with a man of about her own age and station. They were apparently having breakfast. In the other was Gaudriol, shorn of his disguise, and drumming nervously on the table with his long fingers.

Pollard entered the cubicle nearest the door, where he was able to watch the newcomers, and also keep his eye on Gaudriol. From the Chinese youth who appeared from the kitchen to serve him he ordered ham and eggs and a pot of tea.

Gaudriol drew suddenly back and attempted to conceal himself against the wall of his cubicle, and Pollard looked towards the door with interest. The newcomer who had caused Gaudriol such surprise was a tall, slim man, protected from the sharp morning air by a heavy coat with an astrakhan collar. He had a shrewd, mobile face, and by his somewhat eccentric attire, suggested he could perhaps be an artist, an actor, or a poet.

The half-caste nodded to him familiarly, and he passed through the door at the back with a hearty 'Good morning' as a reply to the nod.

The young couple finished their breakfast, while Pollard and Gaudriol sat waiting. The Frenchman was writing a letter of some sort, and wrinkling his brows in deep thought over his task. Pollard forced his ham and eggs into whatever crevices remained inside him after the gigantic meal that the affable Annie had given him, and watched the cracksman out of the corner of his eye.

He realised that Gaudriol was waiting for someone, and that the stranger in the big coat had given him an unpleasant shock.

The door opened again, and a tall, dark individual limped in. Pollard's trained eye noted the limp, and he considered where he had seen just such an infirmity before.

The tall man seated himself by Gaudriol, and the two conversed openly in ordinary tones. Their conversation would have meant nothing to the casual listener, but to Pollard, who had been well coached in the events of the case in hand by Crane, it conveyed a great deal.

'You arrived very late last night,' drawled the stranger, ordering a cup of tea and some toast. 'It must have been very nearly eleven o'clock.'

'I had a lot to do,' said Gaudriol. 'How is everybody?'

The stranger stirred his tea.

'Much the same as ever,' he replied. 'Jones and Smith are in America, and Baldy has gone to France. Simpson, Lees, and Everett are all away on holiday.'

'I met Simpson and Everett,' said Gaudriol. 'Has much happened since I have been away?'

The other considered the matter for some moments, doubtless deciding how best to cloak his words.

'There's a new turn on at the Coliseum, he said, 'named Pearl. An extraordinary show! No one can get to the bottom of it. But I'll tell you more about it some other time. How is your wife?'

The Frenchman's face set grimly.

'She is dead!' he said quietly.

'But, my dear fellow!' A hand went out and was laid sympathetically on his shoulder. 'I — we never knew! How did it happen? When?'

'The night before last,' was the reply. 'Here in London. She was murdered!'

The other started and looked apprehensively around.

'That's a terrible thing to say,' he cautioned his companion. 'It may lead to so much trouble. What happened? Can you tell me?'

Gaudriol shrugged his shoulders.

'I may some day, but for the present it is enough to tell you that she was poisoned. Certain people once threatened to injure me. You know who I mean. Tell me frankly — you have always been my best friend — do you think any of them capable of it?'

For a moment the two men were silent. Pollard drank his coffee noisily and lit a cheap cigarette. He realised that Gaudriol was carrying out Crane's instructions and looking up his old friends. The tall man with a limp seemed in something of a quandary, and Pollard reasoned that his presence was not aiding the Frenchman, for his companion was evidently too cautious to say anything so long as Pollard remained there. With an affected air of nonchalance he slouched over to the half-caste and paid for his breakfast. He felt the eyes of the two men on him as he moved, but he studiously avoided turning towards them.

He collected his change, and was about to leave the restaurant when he heard a cry from beyond the closed door to the back premises.

'Help! Help!'

It was a man's voice that shouted, a

man's voice hoarse with terror and agony. On the spur of the moment Pollard sprang forward. The half-caste attempted to block the door, but a well-timed left, with the full force of Pollard's strength behind it, sent him crashing across his counter. The door was unlocked, and Pollard sped recklessly through it. He could hear footsteps behind him, and he realised that Gaudriol and his companion were after him. The door at the end of the narrow passage was open, and Pollard could see a pile of lumber.

He remembered what Gaudriol had told Crane about the secret room in the Canton.

Once inside the room he hesitated. The rubbish — old barrels, empty wooden cases, and lengths of tarpaulin rolled up — reached to the ceiling. Pollard knew that there was a door past it, but there was no clue to its whereabouts. Somewhere beyond that strange wall he could hear a man moaning; but the wall formed a well-nigh impassable barrier.

Pollard seized a box and pulled it from the pile. If necessary, he would demolish the heap, bit by bit.

But Gaudriol was behind him. Without hesitation the Frenchman seized on the leg of a broken armchair that formed part of the heap, and pulled outwards, disclosing the door. Followed by Pollard and the man with a limp, he dashed into the room that was disclosed.

'My God!' gasped Pollard.

The man in the heavy overcoat was stretched on the floor with blood welling from a wound in his head. Pollard and Gaudriol bent anxiously over him. In the excitement of the moment both forgot the parts that they were playing. All the French in Gaudriol came to the top and he muttered a string of excitable exclamations in his native tongue, while Pollard ran expert hands over the still form.

He breathed a sigh of relief.

'It's all right,' he said. 'He's only stunned.'

Gaudriol rose slowly to his feet. He looked curiously at Pollard. The young man's voice did not accord with his attire.

'Better see who he is,' continued Pollard, heedless of all save the man before him. He felt in a breast pocket and brought out a handsome Morocco-leather case. Each of the cards inside bore the name:

Winbutt Harley,
The Stage Club,
Piccadilly.

★　★　★

Crane managed to calm Mrs. Lamb and walked thoughtfully out into Kensington. He hailed a taxi, and told the driver to take him to the street off Harrow Road in which the Pearler had had his lair. He decided that he would interview the cook, who had been so useful before, with regard to the Pearler's car, and then return to Welbeck Street to await a message from Pollard.

He knew how efficient and reliable Pollard was, but it always worried Crane when the young man was away on his own. The bond of affection between the two was very strong, and Crane knew that in the Stealer they had a dangerous and desperate adversary, who would stick at nothing. The man must know that he was being driven into a corner, and the murder of Greene showed the lengths to which he would go when he found himself in such a position.

Crane was leaning forward to warn his driver to stop, when he noticed that there was a taxi drawn up by Number Fourteen. He rapped on the window to indicate to his driver that he was to draw up by the curb, and peered cautiously ahead.

A tall, thin man in a long dark overcoat was knocking at Number Fourteen. He turned suddenly and hurried back to his cab. Crane could see his face plainly, very white and drawn, with a panic-stricken look about the eyes.

'Harley,' he muttered. 'Now, what is he doing here?'

It was a simple matter to follow the actor's taxi in its journey eastwards, for he was apparently too agitated to tell his driver to take any precautions. But, as is often the case, the very simplicity of the task set him made Crane's man careless; and after a block in the traffic, the taxi in front had disappeared. There were plenty of side-turnings around the spot where they were, and Crane realised ruefully that the quarry might have turned up any one of them.

'I am sorry, sir,' pleaded the driver. 'I never thought he'd slip away like that.'

Crane did not reply. A street name on the wall facing him had attracted his attention. Water Causeway.

He remembered what Gaudriol had said about the Canton Chop-suey and its secret room. The Stealer had been wont to meet his gang there. Harley had been to number fourteen, evidently in search of the Stealer. What more likely than that he was heading for the Canton?

Crane gave the necessary instructions to his taxi driver, and they found their way to the restaurant.

'Wait for me,' ordered Crane, and entered through the swing door. The place was in great disorder, and a half-caste youth was rising slowly from the floor, with one hand to his face. Through the door by him Crane could hear the sound of voices, so with but a casual look at the dazed Oriental, he hurried through and made his way along a passage.

At the far end was a room with the door open. The secret door in the lumber room was swinging on its hinges, and Crane could see Gaudriol bending over a still figure. Beside him stood a seedy-looking youth, whom Crane recognised to his relief as Pollard.

He hurried forward, and as he did so Harley opened his eyes and moaned.

13

Harley's silence

Gaudriol made no comment at the arrival of Lionel Crane. Instead, he stepped forward and aided Crane and Pollard to lift Harley up and make him comfortable. The man with a limp slipped unostentatiously from the room immediately on the entrance of the detective, but Crane studiously ignored him.

He had promised Gaudriol that he would not take unfair advantage of the cracksman's confidence, and he guessed that the man who had feared to meet him was an old associate of Gaudriol's, who knew Crane by sight.

Harley revived slowly, with the aid of some brandy from Crane's flask, and Pollard fetched some water from the restaurant and bathed his head.

'What happened?' Crane asked.

Gaudriol gave vent to his expressive shrug.

'I do not know,' he said. 'I was in here to meet a friend, and this man — Mr. Harley, who was one of the party at Chiswick last night — entered and came straight in here. I was surprised, but felt that I could do nothing. Then this youth,' with a nod at Pollard, 'dashed into here. He had been sitting at a table not far from me in the restaurant. As he opened the door, I heard a man crying out, so came to see what was happening, and what I could do.'

'Well, Harry?' asked Crane, turning to his assistant and covertly warning him to use caution in what he said.

'I came here, Li, to make inquiries, as you told me to,' explained the young man, 'and sat at a table in the restaurant. Mr. Gaudriol was there when I came in, but I remembered that he had said that he would look up his old companions, so I did not warn him who I was. Then this man came in. He walked straight through here. He seemed to be known to the fellow at the counter.

'It struck me that my presence was hindering Mr. Gaudriol, so I came to the counter to pay. While I was doing so, I heard a cry from in here. We had just got the door open when you arrived.'

'So it is your partner, Mr. Crane?' muttered the Frenchman, suspicion clouding his eyes for a moment. 'Why was he sent here?'

'Because I hoped that the Stealer would come here,' replied Crane readily. 'I had an idea that something of this sort might happen, so sent my assistant down to hang around this place.'

Gaudriol seemed satisfied, for he smiled.

'Well, I think we have the Stealer by the heels now,' he declared. 'A well-known actor! It seems strange, doesn't it?'

Crane shook his head doubtfully and bent over Harley who had opened his eyes and was looking dully at those around him.

'There is more in it than that, Gaudriol,' he said. Gaudriol was about to reply, but Harley began speaking.

'Mr. Crane! I — I am glad that you

came.' He looked round apprehensively. 'Was — was there anyone here when you came?'

'These two,' replied Crane, indicating Gaudriol and Pollard.

'Oh! Was that really all? And — ' his eyes studied Pollard, 'when you came into this room, was — was I alone?'

Pollard nodded.

'Yes.'

The actor sank back quietly. Pollard could have sworn that he gave a sigh of relief.

Crane touched Harley's arm.

'Can you tell me what you were doing here?' he asked. 'It is a strange place for a man like you to come to.'

Harley smiled. The cloud had gone from his shrewd eyes, and he chuckled audibly as he looked at Crane.

'Actors do queer things,' he muttered. 'I have always been given to strange haunts. I have had many a good meal here. The proprietor was a friend of mine in my early days. I came to see him.'

Crane frowned, and his stern eyes made Harley colour slightly and look away. One of his hands was clenching and unclenching itself nervously; but the smile did not leave his face.

'But who attacked you?' put in Pollard. 'How did you get this blow on the head?'

'It was an accident,' was the reply.

'But — '

Crane signalled to Pollard and Gaudriol to leave him alone with Harley. Gaudriol hesitated a moment, then he and Pollard went out into the restaurant. Crane turned to the actor with a brow like a thundercloud.

'You must realise, Mr. Harley,' he said shortly, 'that you are in a difficult position. To put it bluntly, you were present last night when the Rose Pearl was stolen, and now you are — discovered in a very shady locality, which is known to be a rendezvous for the Phantom Stealer and his men.'

The actor forced a laugh.

'You mean that you suspect me of being the Stealer?' he asked.

Crane shook his head.

'No, I do not quite think that,' he replied; 'but I do think that you could tell me who the Stealer is. You more than suspect the truth yourself.'

Harley did not reply at once. The smile had left his face, and traces of a great inward struggle were visible.

'It is so very necessary,' continued the detective, 'that the man responsible for so many despicable crimes should be run to earth. I feel sure that you will agree with me in this, and will do all in your power to help me.'

Harley shook his head. His voice was troubled when he replied, but there was no hesitation.

'I cannot tell you anything,' he said. 'There is a certain code that I have always tried to live up to. To betray — to tell you what you ask would be an offence against this code. An offence that I do not wish to make.'

'But, in so serious a case,' Crane's tone was very serious. 'Remember, the man is a murderer!'

Harley winced.

'That is a terrible word to use, Mr. Crane. A desperate man in a trap — cornered, might take a human life in the terror of the moment. Would that be murder?'

Crane inclined his head.

'In the eyes of the law it would,' he replied quietly, 'and, unless the provocation was of a very extraordinary nature, we can but agree with the law.'

'But, the woman — '

'I am not thinking of the woman. The Stealer did not kill her. It is of the detective-sergeant from Scotland Yard that I am thinking. This man was doing his duty. He had followed the Stealer to his lair, and the man killed him. It was done needlessly, Mr. Harley. I grant you that it was done in the heat and panic of the moment but it was a despicable crime nevertheless.'

Harley's lips trembled.

'Don't press me!' he begged. 'I cannot tell you anything — not yet! I may be making a terrible mistake. Until I am convinced, I must keep my own counsel. I will tell you one thing. I was attacked here in this room by a personal friend, whom I surprised waiting for — I don't know what!'

'You suspected this friend of being the Stealer?' asked Crane. 'For that reason you went to his lair, but found that he had flown.'

The colour left Harley's face, and he stared in horror at the detective.

'How much do you know?' he asked, in what was nothing more than a horrified whisper.

'I know that you went to Number Fourteen Elton Road today to interview the Stealer, to prove whether what you had discovered was indeed the truth. He was not there, so you came on here. You had been here before, as you said, so you walked through to this room. He was here, and he attacked you; or else, he was not here — but you were attacked from behind. That is more likely what happened.

'You do not know who attacked you. You have not yet discovered whether your friend is indeed the Stealer. But you know the truth in your heart — '

'Stop!' Harley lifted a shaking hand. 'I do not know how you work, Mr. Crane, but you are uncanny. Don't say anything more about my actions. You seem to know everything. There is one thing only that I want to hear you say. Whom do you suspect of being the Stealer?'

The eyes of the two men met, and Harley's face blanched.

'You — you think — '

Crane nodded.

'Now,' he continued, 'will you tell me what you know?'

But it was of no use. Harley had fainted.

Crane was about to bend over the unconscious man, when he heard voices outside in the restaurant.

'But Harley's here!' cried Malcolm Page's voice. 'He 'phoned asking me to collect both Frayne and Wilson if I could and meet him here.'

Footsteps sounded in the passage, and the author entered, followed closely by Wilson, Pollard and Gaudriol.

Page gave a cry of concern when he saw Harley, and hurried over to him.

'Who's done this? Is he dead?'

'No,' said Crane reassuringly. 'He is merely unconscious. He has had a very severe shock. He will be all right shortly.'

Page placed a hand on his friend's heart and nodded at Wilson.

'It's beating,' he affirmed. 'Slow but steady. Now, I wonder what he wanted us to come here for?'

'Some funny business,' declared the journalist in reply. 'But the thing is who gave him that awful blow on the head?'

'This was the weapon,' interposed Crane, holding out a heavy metal bar. 'It is what our criminal friends refer to as a 'flosher'.'

Page inspected it with a shudder.

'What a murderous instrument!' he exclaimed. 'Poor old Harley! One of the best.'

'I cannot understand anyone trying to do Harley in!' put in Wilson. 'He was the kindest-hearted fellow living. He couldn't have had an enemy. He was the sort of chap who can see good in anything. If a fellow was to punch him on the nose, he wouldn't blame the aggressor, but would worry himself ill wondering in what way he had upset the chap. He would decide that he deserved what he got, because he must have been very aggravating. A dear old man, Harley, one of the old school. Very rigid about his personal code of honour, and all that. We've ragged him frequently, eh, Page?'

Page smiled.

'He always takes it so well. 'You chaps see things one way, I another', he always says. It's a pity more of us don't try to live up to Harley's code of honour.'

All the while that the two friends were talking, Crane's keen eyes noted the agitation that was moving both of them. Their minds were not on what they were saying, and their eyes roved the small room anxiously. The detective was not surprised when Page repeated Harley's question.

'When you found Harley,' he asked, 'was — was anyone — his assailant here?'

Crane shook his head, and once again Pollard received the impression that the reply was received with a sigh of relief. The young man looked to his chief for instructions. He expected Crane to attempt to force the reason for their agitation from the two men, but the detective merely smiled quietly and signalled to Gaudriol.

'Had we better get Harley off to bed?' asked Page.

'Yes; and I want you to take him to Welbeck Street. Pollard will go with you. Pollard, I want you to stay with Mr. Harley. You will have to guard him. The Stealer will know soon that his murderous attack did not kill the man who has stumbled on to his secret, and may make a second attempt.'

Page gasped, the shade of apprehension crossing his face again.

'I never thought of that!' he exclaimed. 'Do you think it likely, Crane?'

'I do.'

'May I — we — stay and help guard him at your place?' interposed Wilson. 'We have an appointment to meet you at Welbeck Street at five this evening. May we wait there for you today, and guard Harley in the meantime?'

Crane gave his consent willingly, so the two friends carried Harley tenderly out to a taxi and drove away, accompanied by Pollard.

'There's something very fishy about those men,' muttered Gaudriol, when he was alone with Crane. 'They all know more than they will tell. I cannot understand it.'

'Sit down a moment, Gaudriol,' said Crane. 'I think that we have earned a smoke, and I have some questions to ask you.'

The ex-convict drew out a pipe, and accepted a fill from the detective's pouch. The two lit their pipes in silence. Gaudriol was watching Crane's face, and Crane was preparing what he had to say.

'Well, Mr. Crane?'

'I have discovered the murderer of your wife, Gaudriol.'

The Frenchman sprang to his feet with a hoarse exclamation. His hands clenched spasmodically, and the veins stood out on his forehead. With an effort he calmed himself and sank down again.

'I'm sorry,' he muttered. 'It came as such a shock. Tell me — who is it?'

'Among your former associates,' went on Crane quietly, 'there was a tall, dark man with brown eyes, who walked with a decided limp.'

Gaudriol nodded.

'He was — still is — my lieutenant. My best friend.'

'Your worst enemy,' contradicted Crane. 'He killed your wife!'

Gaudriol made no outcry, but puffed stolidly at his pipe. His eyes rested thoughtfully on Crane's face.

'Either you are playing with me, Mr. Crane,' he asserted, 'or you have been misled. There was no cause for Limpy Latimer to kill Madeleine. They were like brother and sister!'

'That may be, but listen, and I will tell you what I have learnt today. You can draw your own conclusions.'

As Crane recounted the story that had been told to him by the kitchen aid at the Devon Hotel, Gaudriol ceased smoking. A crease appeared between his eyes, and his long jaw set wickedly. Towards the end he was breathing heavily, and his eyes flashed fire.

'I'll kill him!' he snarled. 'Crane — you are a just man! Am I not justified in killing him?'

The strong hand of the detective closed

on Gaudriol's arm, and the steady grip aided him to regain his self-control.

'One can't take the law into one's own hands in a case like this, Gaudriol. Rest assured that he will pay the full penalty. But, are you sure that it is the man that you are thinking of?'

'Yes. I can see much that I did not understand now. Limpy stirred up all that ill-feeling at my trial. He let the yarn get around that I was double-crossing the gang. The men had always found me square, but when my own lieutenant accused me, what else could they think? But, why should he do it? Why?'

Gaudriol turned for the door like a mad thing.

'He was here when you came in!' he snapped. 'That was him! Come with me, Mr. Crane, and we will accuse him to his face!'

'But he's gone!' exclaimed Crane. 'Where will we find him?'

The Frenchman did not hesitate, although it meant exposing another of his secret haunts.

'At Mrs. Lamb's, a boarding-house in

Kensington. He has lived there for years.'

'I was at Mrs. Lamb's this morning,' declared Crane. 'I went there to find you.'

'Then you will have seen Limpy, for he is always much in evidence,' he laughed grimly. 'He is her star boarder, for he passes himself off as a retired colonel — Colonel Bore-Talkington!'

14

The plot against Gaudriol

On the way to Kensington, both Crane and Gaudriol took steps to disguise themselves, so that they would not be recognised by Limpy Latimer at first sight.

'He always sits in the window by the front door,' explained Gaudriol. 'If he saw us coming up the steps, he'd bolt at once. As it is, he will take us for two prospective boarders.'

Out of the corner of his eye Crane saw the bluff colonel at the window, peering over the top of his paper, as Gaudriol pressed the bell. When they were admitted to the hall, and Mrs. Lamb came forward to interview them, the colonel drifted out to take a look at them.

'I am sorry to worry you,' explained Crane, 'but this is the gentleman that we wish to speak to.'

He indicated the colonel, who stared doubtfully at them. But Gaudriol stepped up to him and snarled in a low voice:

'If you make a break for it, I'll squeal, Limpy! We want a few words with you.'

Fear showed plainly in the man's eyes, and he seemed on the point of cutting and running for it. But he controlled himself with an obvious effort, and turned to Mrs. Lamb.

'I don't know these — er — gentlemen, but I suppose that I must hear what they have to say!' he blustered. 'We will not be disturbed in the smoking room, eh?'

'No, colonel, I will see that no one goes near there.' She turned icily to the others. 'If you follow Colonel Bore-Talkington, he will show you the smoking room in which you can discuss your business.'

Gaudriol did not follow Colonel Bore-Talkington. He walked beside him, and his grip on the bluff colonel's arm was like a vice. He thrilled to feel the man trembling under his touch, and to know that at last he had the murderer of his wife in his grasp, and that the man was suffering the most acute agonies of fear.

In the smoking room, a dingy, thread-bare apartment, Limpy Latimer — no longer the bluff retired colonel, but a trembling mass of nerves — sank into a chair. Gaudriol stood over him, his eyes blazing, and his face working with emotion. Crane stationed himself behind the Frenchman, ready to restrain him if his passion overwhelmed him.

'Limpy,' snarled Gaudriol, 'you killed Madeleine!'

Latimer wet his lips nervously, and his knuckles showed white as he gripped the arms of his chair.

He conjured up a shaky laugh.

'Why, Paul, don't be absurd!' he blustered weakly. 'Me kill Madeleine! Why, you know what pals we were, she and I!'

'There's no sense in lying!' The Frenchman swung round on Crane. 'This is Lionel Crane, Limpy. Ah! You might well wince! You didn't know that he was after you, did you? Mr. Crane, tell him what we know.'

In a quiet, almost toneless voice Crane repeated the story of the servant at the

Devon Hotel. He sketched her meeting with the man at the cinema, who later became engaged to her. In detail, and with great dramatic force, he described the actions of the murderer on the day when he put the arsenic in the milk.

Limpy Latimer sat slouched in his chair throughout, his eyes on the floor, the arms of the chair alone keeping him from falling forward.

'Well, Limpy?'

It was Gaudriol who spoke, and the words rasped unpleasantly. The Frenchman was trembling now, and the sweat was standing out on his forehead in beads. Crane laid a restraining hand on his arm, and he struggled for composure.

Limpy looked up, and indicated Crane.

'He's lying, Paul,' he declared. 'He hopes, by making you and I quarrel, to break the gang. Can't you see that?'

Gaudriol's lips drew back in a derisive snarl, and only Crane's grip on his arm kept him from striking the man before him.

'Shall I fetch the girl from the Devon?' the detective suggested quietly.

'You've squared her!' sneered Limpy.

'I have not squared her,' was the reply. 'Gaudriol, will you ring the Devon and ask them to send the kitchen maid Mary here at once!'

Latimer laughed wildly.

'I told you so, Paul — he's lying! The girl at the Devon was named Pearl!'

'How do you know?'

Latimer never answered the sharp question, for he had realised his own slip the moment that the words were said. Crane had taken a long chance, banking on the strained condition of the man's nerves, and he had plunged blindly into the trap. His face went ashen, and he fumbled for words, but the fight was out of him.

'Now, Limpy,' demanded Gaudriol, 'why did you kill Madeleine?'

'Because she knew too much!' The words poured out hysterically, and there was now no attempt at concealment. 'I was going to sell you, because I hated you! I always do the work for you, and you and Madeleine grab the lion's share. The gang would follow me if you were out of it for good. When you came out this time, I had doped it all out, Paul, that it would be for a very short time. You were going back for a long time — as a 'lifer'.

'There are many like me who hate you, for you treat us like dirt, and you're too finicky. We know that you gave Rod Dewe up for the Porter murder. You sold him, because you said that you did not hold with murder, and that Rod deserved what he got. Rod was my pal, Paul. Do you begin to understand, now?

'We made up our minds that we would put you up for life. I was to meet you this morning and take you — somewhere. The boys were waiting there. Matters would come to a showdown. We intended to give Ford his. He is a snitch, and has had it coming for a long time. You would have been found alone with the body, and enough evidence to hang you ten times over. We weren't working for a hanging, though. We wanted you out of the way for good. Now do you understand?'

Gaudriol nodded slowly.

'What about Madeleine?' he asked.

'She got on to my track. How, I don't know! Call it woman's intuition if you like, but she saw through the game. I killed her before she could warn you. Now you know!'

Crane frowned, and took up the cross-examination.

'You say that Madeleine Gaudriol discovered your plan, and so you killed her. That does not quite fit in with the crime. If you killed her to prevent her exposing you, you would have shot her, or stabbed her the moment that you learnt of her knowledge. As it is, you spent more than a week cultivating the girl at the Devon, and then you made two attempts to poison Madeleine Gaudriol. In other words, you were in no hurry to kill her, but could take your time.'

'It was three weeks ago,' replied Limpy, 'that I noticed that Madeleine was getting suspicious. I realised then that I would have to kill her before she learnt anything of importance and passed it on to her husband. I started to put my plan into operation right away. I killed her the day before Gaudriol was released because I found that she knew more than I had at first suspected. Otherwise, it was my intention to wait until the morning milk yesterday.'

He sat back quietly as he finished speaking. He had completely regained his self-control and faced Gaudriol calmly. Crane touched the Frenchman's arm.

'Ring Scotland Yard, will you, Gaudriol, and ask Detective-Inspector Herrick to come along right away? Tell him that we've got the murderer of your wife. Then, if you'll come along to Welbeck Street with me we'll have a pick-me-up, and some lunch. You can't do anything with regard to Latimer. The matter must rest with the law, but he'll get his just deserts, I promise you that.'

Gaudriol shrugged expressively.

'You know best, Mr. Crane,' he muttered. 'But — ' His fists clenched, and Latimer shrank from the blaze in his eyes. Then the Frenchman turned and hurried from the room.

Back at his chambers, Crane mixed a stiff drink for Gaudriol and insisted on his drinking it. The Frenchman would eat no food, but obeyed the detective's order that he go up to Pollard's room and attempt to get some sleep.

'The place is turning into a hospital, Li,' chuckled Pollard. 'Harley in your bed, with Page standing guard with a double-barrelled shotgun, and now Gaudriol in my downy couch. Make some people raise their eyebrows, what — famous cracksman asleep in detective's bed!'

Crane smiled absentmindedly.

'I want you to look after them all, Harry,' he warned the young man. 'I'm going out again. If any message comes through, I am going first to the Countess of Wigmouth's place, and then to Scotland Yard. Herrick should have some information with regard to that camp furniture.'

Crane had not been gone many minutes when Frayne turned up.

'I only received your 'phone message fifteen minutes ago,' he explained to Page. 'I went down to Canton at once, and found old Li Chang in an awful stew at the commotion that had happened. Chinamen are not supposed to show their feelings, but our old friend was well-nigh weeping when he told me that Lionel Crane had been down there. It has killed his trade. No more crooks will take advantage of the room at the back now that Crane knows of it.

'I heard from him that you had come on to Crane's place, so I followed. Now, enlighten me, what on earth has happened? What's all the fuss about?'

Page took him up to the room where Harley was and gave him a full account of what had occurred. Harley had recovered, but would say nothing to anyone. He lay on the bed and peered doubtingly at all around him. Pollard began to wonder whether the blow on his head had affected his brain, for if any one of his friends approached close to him he shrank away with an extraordinary expression on his face.

When Frayne came, Harley gave no sign of recognition, and made no comment during the recital of the morning's adventures.

'Poor old Harley!' boomed the actor; 'but what on earth happened, old chap?'

He bent over the bed and smiled at his fellow-actor, but Harley shrank away as before.

'Here, Harley, you know who it is,' pleaded Frayne. 'You haven't forgotten me — Walle Frayne?'

Harley shook his head as he divined the suspicion in Frayne's mind.

'I have forgotten no one,' he affirmed. 'My brain is quite clear. I have received a very great shock. My faith in human nature has been well-nigh destroyed. For that reason, I wish to speak to no one until I have had a few more words with Lionel Crane.'

'But, my dear Harley — '

'Don't press me, Frayne. I must speak to Crane first.'

Frayne moved away from the bed with a shrug. Pollard, who had stationed himself on a chair by Harley's head, nodded encouragingly at the injured man.

'That's it, Mr. Harley,' he exclaimed. 'You wait until the chief comes. He'll sort things out for you.'

Page went off shortly afterwards to help himself to a drink, Pollard quietly asking him to fetch it for himself. The young man had had a few words with Gaudriol, and the cracksman had warned him to sit by Harley's bed, and not leave his position on any pretext.

'The Stealer might make an attempt to get him again,' the Frenchman explained.

'But his friends — ' Pollard had replied.

Gaudriol had merely shrugged expressively, and Pollard had obeyed him without another word. Like Crane, he realised that Gaudriol was 'white', and would harm no man. He stole from those who could afford to lose because he had made stealing his profession. Something about him made Pollard trust and obey him.

Grumbling to himself, Linker brought lunch up to the bedrooms and the meal was eaten in silence.

The evening wore on, but at a quarter to five Crane and Herrick walked in.

'Ah, here's Crane!' boomed Frayne. 'Now for an explanation. We've been waiting for you all day, Crane. Your assistant wouldn't let us go away. Not that we wanted to. I for one am too interested to hear what you have to say. Are you going to tell us who the Stealer is?'

Crane nodded, and looked quietly round at the tense, expectant faces.

'I will tell you everything in a few minutes,' he declared. 'But first I want you to call Gaudriol, Harry. Then I want to inform everyone that there are police officers around this building, and that any attempt at a break for freedom will be vain. The Phantom Stealer is cornered.'

Frayne laughed in huge glee.

'I like that!' he cried. 'That means that he is in this room.'

Each man looked doubtfully at his neighbour, while Harley closed his eyes and sank back on to his pillows. His face was terrible, and could not have been more ghastly had Crane pronounced his death warrant.

15

The truth at last

'I am going to take you back to the beginning,' began Crane, seating himself so that he could observe all his audience — 'to the moment when the Stealer first started his campaign to secure the pearl from the Devon Hotel. He had discovered, as a result of some incautious word let drop by one of Gaudriol's former associates, that Mrs. Gaudriol — or Madame Bourchaud, as she was calling herself — had the Andapore Pearl in her possession, and he made up his mind to make it his.

'He concealed himself in her room on a night that seemed propitious to his plans at a moment between twelve and half-past. We can definitely set the time, as we find that Mrs. Gaudriol was taken ill shortly after drinking milk supplied to her at four o'clock and retired to her room. She did not leave it again until shortly after twelve, when she came down to the hall at my request, because I wanted to ask her a few questions.'

'What were you doing there, if I might ask?' put in Page.

'The police had received warning through the usual channels that the Stealer intended to make a haul at the Devon, and Inspector Herrick asked me to lend a hand.'

Page nodded and helped himself to a cigarette. Each of the men was watching Crane intently, with the exception of Harley. The eyes of the older man were still closed, and he seemed to be paying no attention to the proceedings.

'Shortly after the unfortunate woman returned to her room, she drank the milk which it was her custom to take at eleven o'clock, but which she delayed taking on account of the upset caused apparently by the glass that she had taken at four o'clock. Both these glasses of milk, I have proved already, were dosed with arsenic, the second containing a fatal dose.'

'The Stealer!' exclaimed Wilson, but

Crane shook his head.

'No; this was an enemy of Gaudriol's, who is already in the hands of the police and will undoubtedly pay the full penalty for his despicable crime. The Stealer had nothing to do with the poisoning, which, in effect, nearly upset his plans.

'As she placed the tumbler down, on taking her milk, the Stealer must have advanced on her and seized her from behind by the throat. The pressure was judiciously placed to render her unconscious, but do no lasting harm.

'Imagine his horror, when the woman commenced to writhe with agony and suffer from terrible sickness, even while he held her. To cover the noise, he snored forcefully, and managed to deceive the detective who was stationed outside the window.

'After events have proved that the Stealer was of an excitable nature. Still gripping the poor woman by the throat, he got her over to her bed. When he released his hold, to his horror she was dead. The man must have suffered agonies as he looked down on the dead woman, one of her hands clutching the chain around her neck. The bag that had hung at the other end of that chain was already in his possession, for he had broken the chain in his struggle with her.

'We can picture him pushing the pearl that had cost so much into his pocket, all the while keeping up the effect of someone sleeping heavily and noisily. I am inclined to think that he was aware of the police cordon around the building, and had a cut-and-dried plan to work on, but, even with this, it must have been a terrible task to dress himself in some of his victim's clothes, clean up the traces in the room, and then, having hidden the body under the bed, to sit in a chair for the remainder of the night and snore at intervals. I want to impress upon you the strain which the man was undergoing because it bears a great deal on after events.'

Crane looked quietly around as he spoke. One member of his audience was pale and twitching behind an air of forced indifference. This man opened his mouth as though to speak, but Crane shook his head at him and went on relentlessly with his reconstruction of events.

'A few minutes after six in the morning the Stealer opened the door of the room and saw Inspector Herrick and myself, who had spent the night on the landing. He closed the door again, pulled down the veil that he had placed over his hat, and braced his nerves. Then he walked past us with averted head, and away from the hotel.

'He must have known that he would be followed, and he must have conceived a plan as he went along. He lured Detective-Sergeant Greene into Kensal Green Cemetery and knocked him out. Then he hid at some convenient spot and divested himself of his disguise. He had a lair nearby — Number Fourteen, Elton Road — so he made his way there and changed.'

Crane's eyes rested thoughtfully on Page, who fidgeted nervously with a cigarette.

'Then,' went on Crane, 'he went to pay a very early call on a man with whom he had contrived to get very intimate. He found this friend gloating over an addition to his collection, and spent some few minutes admiring the pearl that the friend showed to him. He then claimed an appointment, and told his friend not to trouble to come to the door with him, as he knew the way perfectly. I am right in that, aren't I, Page? You did not go down to the door with him?'

'He — he went down alone,' stammered Page, scarcely able to get the words out on account of his agitation.

He looked nervously towards Herrick, who had shifted his position and had been reinforced by a plainclothes man, who stood by him not far from Harley's bed.

'I thought that that was what happened,' declared Crane. 'For your housekeeper assured me that she admitted a visitor, but that he did not pass out of the front door until after you had gone running out, because she stopped to speak to a friend who was passing at the time when she admitted him.'

'But — ' began Page.

'He only went as far as the lobby off

your hall, Page,' explained Crane. 'There he donned his mask, and returned to your study. The pearl that you showed him had aroused the greed for pearls that has always been his downfall.

'He attacked you and you dashed out of the house and round to my place. Meanwhile, the Stealer realised that suspicion might fall upon him, as he had been your last visitor. So he proceeded to lay a false trail. He went to the library and fetched the steps. He made a fatal error, for he underrated my experience. I suspected the prints in your study the moment that I saw them. They were too obvious. And up on the roof there were in reality two trails leading to the rainwater pipe, but one had been very carefully obliterated. Then, again, you assured me that the library steps had never been used in your study before, and yet there was the plain trail of the wheels from the library door to a position under the skylight and back again.

'In some ways the Stealer has been extremely careless,' continued Crane. 'He sent the workmen away from the base of the rainwater pipe so that if we traced him as far as that we would jump to the conclusions that that was when the ascent to the roof was made, but he did not pay sufficient attention to details. The smuts on that pipe were undisturbed. It was evident to anyone who cared to make a careful study that no one had climbed it.'

Crane paused for a few moments, but no one spoke. All were eyeing him intently, enthralled by his recital.

'We now come to the murder of the Scotland Yard man,' Crane continued. 'He had left the clothes that he had taken from Mrs. Gaudriol's room in the cemetery, so during the afternoon he donned a favourite disguise — the same that he had worn when he spoke to the workmen by Page's place — and returned to Kensal Green. He retrieved the clothing and took it back with him to Number Fourteen, Elton Road. As he entered the house he realised that he had been followed.

'His nerves were on edge from the ghastly experiences of the night before, for, although he had stolen on many occasions, he had always worked in a clever, quiet way, and had never before come up against death. The shock of the woman dying in his hands was enough to turn his brain. Be that as it may, he lost his head when he realised that the police had traced him to his lair, and so he set upon Sergeant Greene, and killed him.

'At the same pitch of hysterical excitement, he took the body and placed it in the cemetery. Doubtless he hoped by this to throw the police off the scent, and to make matters more certain, he made a grave error, for from the clues on Greene's body, Herrick and I were able to find our way to the Elton Road house, and to discover there a great deal concerning the Stealer.

'There was some camp furniture there, into which Herrick made exhaustive inquiries at all the big stores. Even as I expected — for I had gauged the man's character correctly — it had been bought at a big stores by a regular customer. The man was so accustomed to buying things at the stores that when he required camp furniture he simply sent his manservant round to order it.

'Also, from the back of the deckchair, I discovered that he used a peculiar brilliantine. I analysed some fragments of hair in the fingernails of the dead woman at the Devon Hotel, and the same brilliantine was discovered.

'Then there is another point. When Mrs. Gaudriol was struggling with the Stealer, he was wrenching at the chain that was around her neck. The chain left a vivid weal on her skin, showing clearly the rather out of the ordinary pattern — '

All eyes went instinctively to a hand with a neat bandage around it.

'It must have scored the hand of the Stealer — '

'Crane!' It was Wilson who cried out. 'You don't mean — '

Crane nodded to Herrick, and the inspector's heavy hand dropped on to Walle Frayne's shoulder. The plainclothes man stepped forward, and both braced themselves for a struggle.

But Frayne made no movement. He crouched in his chair, his face livid and the hand holding his cigarette shaking spasmodically.

'Go on, Crane,' he muttered. 'I knew that this had to come. I'm glad, in a way. I've had my run. After that night at the Devon, I knew that the end must come. I never banked on things coming to that pitch, I stole for the excitement of the game, and because I coveted the pearls. But I did not expect it to lead to murder. I — I thought I'd killed that woman, and — then there was the detective! The game's up. That's why I have sat here throughout your recital, and made no attempt at a break for freedom. I've lost, and I'm willing to pay.'

He stopped abruptly, and seemed to cast around for words.

'Go on,' he repeated. 'Tell all you know, and then I'll — I'll supplement.'

Harley moaned slightly, and Frayne stretched out a hand and gripped the older man's. He retained his hold as Crane went on with his narrative.

'From Elton Street the Stealer returned to his own flat. He was a quick worker, for he intended to steal still another pearl that night.'

'But,' interrupted Page, 'the Rose Pearl was his. He had bought it.'

Crane shook his head.

'I interviewed the Countess of Wigmouth today. Frayne had made her a very big offer for the pearl. She allowed him to take it, and accepted his cheque, but it was only a provisional sale until she received her husband's consent. Her husband cabled his refusal yesterday morning, and Frayne promised over the 'phone to return the pearl today. He had known all along that his lordship would refuse to sell, because a larger offer had been made to him in India. Frayne knew this, but he wanted the pearl.

'So he arranged to have it stolen while it was in his temporary possession. The account on which his cheque was drawn has not sufficient funds in it to cover the amount. I myself took the cheque to the bank today and had it returned.

'We now,' continued Crane, 'come to the robbery at Frayne's flat. He had in his employ the man Pearson. Pearson

— who, by the way, is now dead — was a strange character who stole to provide an old father with luxuries. Frayne had discovered this, and, by threatening the man with exposure, he got him into his employ as an assistant. The story of Pearson wanting to go straight and all that was, of course, pure imagination. Pearson hated his work, but had not the moral courage to expose Frayne, even when he learnt that he was indeed the Stealer.

'As for the attack at which we were all present, Pearson switched off the lights, and Frayne quietly slipped the pearl back into the secret hiding place of which he had boasted to us. It was in your false teeth, I think, wasn't it, Frayne?'

Frayne nodded, and exposed the hiding place in his dental plate.

'You don't seem to have missed much,' he replied quietly.

'I noticed your slight difficulty in speaking when I first entered,' explained Crane, 'and that you could articulate clearly when you returned with the pearl. It was only a small thing, but it fitted in with your going from the room for a very brief moment before disclosing the pearl to us, and it was the sort of ingenious hiding place that I would have expected from the Phantom Stealer.

'Also you told me freely of your friends' habits; but there was a box of Burma cheroots on your table, and from your account at the stores I discovered that you used a great deal more cognac brandy than is usually drunk. Doubtless you found it necessary to steady your nerves. Then, again, the brilliantine was discovered on your table. I noticed the scent when I entered your bedroom.'

'What about the visiting card that was found after the lights were extinguished for the second time?' asked Wilson.

Crane smiled.

'We were all watching one another at the time,' Wilson exclaimed. 'So it was simple for Frayne to leave the switch. He knew where the cards and the pen and ink were. I see it now!'

But Crane shook his head.

'That would have been the simpler way,' he agreed; 'but from studying the handwriting on that card, and on the fragment of the diary that Herrick retained in his hand, I learnt that Pearson had entered the room while the light was out and written the card. Probably Frayne considered that this would be safer.'

'Why did Pearson run away?' Page asked.

'Because he suffered a sudden revulsion of feeling. Earlier in the evening he had received a great shock. His father had questioned him more closely than usual as to where he obtained his money, and had almost stumbled on to the truth. He had frightened Pearson, and made him realise how precarious his position was. Among other things, the older Pearson had mislaid his watch, and he accused his son of taking it — 'I believe you are a thief, Harry! That's where the money comes from. And now you have taken my watch'!'

Gaudriol nodded quietly. He could understand Pearson's agitation now on the occasion on which he had followed him from Ewe Street.

'Pearson decided to run away from

Frayne, and to leave behind his diary for the police to find. By once more extinguishing the light, Frayne saved himself for a bit longer.'

Once again Crane paused.

'The next incidents I do not quite understand myself. In some way or other Mr. Harley stumbled on to Frayne's secret. He decided rashly that he would warn his friend. For this reason he hurried to Elton Road, only to find that Frayne had left there. From Elton Road he went to the Canton in Water Causeway. I understand that you had frequently met there. Though that also I do not understand, for it is certainly a shady locality.'

'Oh, that was Wilson's stunt,' put in Page. 'We used to meet for bridge every alternate night at Frayne's, and two nights a week we would play in the secret room at the Canton. It made it rather romantic!'

'Wilson showed you the secret room?'

'No. Wilson suggested that we find some weird place to play in, for the fun of it, and Frayne told us of Li Chang and the room behind his restaurant. He was always given to wandering around in odd corners, so we did not think it at all strange his knowing of the place. I should say,' the author added shrewdly, 'that he got a great deal of amusement out of taking us there, and found it very useful as a cloak for his other movements.'

Frayne nodded.

'It used to amuse me,' he confessed; 'and I used to fit in meetings with my men for nights on which we played bridge. I would stay behind after you had gone to meet them.'

Crane turned to Harley, who had been listening intently.

'Will you tell me the truth of your actions today?' he asked.

Harley and Frayne exchanged glances before Harley replied.

'It will serve no purpose if I don't,' decided the old man. 'But first of all, I have something that you must know, Mr. Crane, and you alone. If I might have a pencil, I will write it down for you.'

Pollard handed him the necessary writing materials, and passed the finished

240

note to Crane. Crane gave no sign of surprise when he read the few words, for he had suspected something of the sort. The message was: '*Frayne is my son. It is essential that no one should know this.*'

'You can imagine my feelings, Mr. Crane,' went on the old man, 'when I went to — to Frayne's flat today and discovered, by the merest chance, the book that was snatched from Inspector Herrick's hands last night. It was in the private drawer of his desk, but I had been to the drawer before, so thought nothing of the action today.

'The first words that I opened at confirmed fears that have troubled me for some time. My — Walle Frayne was the Phantom Stealer! The address in Elton Road was given, so, on the spur of the moment, I decided to hurry there. I intended to plead with him to clear out of the country and make a fresh start. I was sinning by doing so, but I think that you will understand.

'He was not there, so I went on to the Canton. I went straight into the secret room. The Stealer was there in his mask.

241

In my agitation I called out, without considering the consequences: 'Walle! I know everything!' I remember nothing else, save that the figure sprang at me, until I revived to find you by me.'

He looked at Frayne, who nodded.

'Yes,' he confessed, 'I hit you. Your accusation was the final straw. I realised that the game was up, and once again I lost my head in the excitement of the moment.'

Father and son looked at one another, then Harley closed his eyes again and turned away. There was no doubt but that the shock of the disclosure had broken the old man up terribly. His fictitious air of youth had dropped away from him, and he looked every one of his years. Crane realised that Harley could not long survive his son's disgrace.

16

The Stealer speaks

Detective Inspector Herrick uttered the time-honoured warning that whatever Frayne said might be used in evidence against him, but the Stealer waved him aside.

'I must speak,' he said. 'It can do me no harm, for I shall plead guilty. I am not afraid to pay for my crimes. Until this last series of episodes I have reaped the full enjoyment out of them. I have proved, however, that crime can never pay. It will for a time, but something always crops up, and then comes the smash. I started because I craved the excitement, and I could not afford to satisfy my desire for pearls; in a way, I treated my operations as a joke; I blinded myself to the seriousness of them; and look what they have led me to!'

He made an expressive gesture, and

was silent for a brief moment.

'A man called Limpy Latimer told me of the Pearl of Andapore,' he continued. 'He hated you, Gaudriol. I may tell you that many of them do. You are too squeamish for them. If you'll take my tip, you'll cut the game now while the going is good. Limpy worked with me once, and he told me of Madame Bourchaud, as she called herself. He alone knew who she was, and that she had the pearl with her. He dared not go after it, for he was too scared of Gaudriol, but I was interested.

'I made a few careful inquiries, and learnt the lay of the land at the Devon by staying there for a week. You will remember that I went to France for a week last month. 'France', in this case, was a room at the Devon.

'My plans were working smoothly, when I heard suddenly that Gaudriol would be out the next afternoon. I realised that I was going to have to speed things up. I paid a visit to the Devon at eight o'clock, but discovered that the lady was in bed ill. It seemed that my plan was to fail. I decided to take a drive, while I thought the problem out, and to make another attempt later. I returned shortly after twelve. You were in the hall, Crane, and so was madame.

'It was the work of a moment for me to nip up to her room and under the bed. Your deductions with regard to my movements were correct, Crane, to the last detail. She returned to her room soon after I had concealed myself. She was very agitated, and drank her milk the moment that she entered. I saw my opportunity while she had her back turned and advanced on her. My horror and dismay, when she collapsed in my hands, you can well imagine! I wonder now that I did not rush screaming from the room. Some force outside myself seemed to actuate me.

'I reasoned that you would have guards around the place, so I tried to cover the sound that she was making by snoring; although it is unlikely that you had your men in position by then. I shall never forget that woman's face as I forced the body under the bed.

'For the rest, I acted pretty much as you described, Crane. The man who followed me to the cemetery I managed to overcome, then I set a crowd on him by telling a woman who passed me that he had tried to grab my purse.

'Page had not told me of his pearl. When I entered and found him toying with it, I was seized with the mad idea to pull off two coups in one day. I failed, as you know. That is to say, I failed to get Page's pearl, although I succeeded with the Rose Pearl in the evening. You were right there also, Crane. My plan was to have the pearl stolen while in my possession, and then stop the cheque and refuse to make any compensation to the countess. It was not my fault that the pearl had been stolen while in my possession. I had witnesses who would swear that my tale of the theft was the true one, That was why I was so pleased when you turned up, Crane. What better witness could I have than a famous detective!'

He shrugged his shoulders.

'It has been a great game,' he decided; 'but the gods have been against me, and the game itself got out of hand. It very much resembled trying to ride a restive horse, which ran away with me, and has now thrown me.'

He shrugged his shoulders again, and a look passed between him and his father.

'Look!' cried the older man excitedly, pointing at the door. The age-old trick was so unexpected that it worked like a charm. Every man in the room swung round towards the door. With a surprising leap, Frayne crossed the room and dived recklessly through the open window, the splintering of the glass being the first real warning that the others received of what had happened.

Pollard was the first to reach the window and peer out.

'He's away!' he cried excitedly. 'He's limping badly, but still he's running.'

'He won't run far,' boomed Herrick, blowing a furious peal on his whistle and gesticulating through the window. 'My men will get him.'

But the Scotland Yard men never got

the Phantom Stealer. He preferred to go to a Higher Court. Even as the detectives closed in on him, he ran forward and flung himself in front of a passing bus.

THE END

We do hope that you have enjoyed reading this large print book.

Did you know that all of our titles are available for purchase?

We publish a wide range of high quality large print books including:
Romances, Mysteries, Classics
General Fiction
Non Fiction and Westerns

Special interest titles available in large print are:
The Little Oxford Dictionary
Music Book, Song Book
Hymn Book, Service Book

Also available from us courtesy of Oxford University Press:
Young Readers' Dictionary
(large print edition)
Young Readers' Thesaurus
(large print edition)

For further information or a free brochure, please contact us at:
Ulverscroft Large Print Books Ltd.,
The Green, Bradgate Road, Anstey,
Leicester, LE7 7FU, England.
Tel: (00 44) **0116 236 4325**
Fax: (00 44) **0116 234 0205**

*Other titles in the
Linford Mystery Library:*

MARKED FOR MURDER

Norman Lazenby

'Leave this affair alone, Martinson — Jean Hallison is dead . . . ' The caller had rung off, leaving Inspector Jim Martinson wondering if this was a bluff. Had Jean been murdered? And where did the suave, grinning Montoni fit in? He was accused of assaulting two women — but at the same time Jim himself had been watching him elsewhere. Now, however, Jim links the chain of evidence — slowly tightening the rope that will bring in the sinister gang that is terrorising Framcastle.